TWO NAMES FOR

"Simply and subtly
knowable characters and plausibly
complex motivations, this won't
disappoint those who recognized Fenwick
in *Murder in Haste* as a possible major
contender."
—Anthony Boucher, *NY Times*

"…a real corker of a classic mystery…
an immensely enjoyable detective novel,
complexly yet cleanly plotted with
characters that actually live (until they
die, that is). For someone who later
excelled at the stripped down mid-
century crime novel, Fenwick here
produced a densely packed true detective
tale with quite credible police
investigation."
—Curtis Evans, *The Passing Tramp*

"[She] can describe the best and worst of a
character in one sentence, and can make
a single gesture tell of years of
accumulated pain or madness…
Fenwick's novels are all beautifully
plotted in human intimacy."
— Carol Cleveland, *Twentieth-Century
Crime and Mystery Writers*

Elizabeth Fenwick Bibliography (1916-1996)

Mysteries:
The Inconvenient Corpse (1943;
  as E. P. Fenwick)
Murder in Haste (1944; as E. P. Fenwick)
Two Names For Death (1945;
  as E. P. Fenwick)
Poor Harriet (1957)
A Long Way Down (1959)
A Friend of Mary Rose (1961)
A Night Run (1961)
The Make-Believe Man (1963)
The Silent Cousin (1966)
The Passenger (1967)
Disturbance on Berry Hill (1968)
Goodbye, Aunt Elva (1968)
Impeccable People (1971)
The Last of Lysandra (1973)

Mainstream Novels:
The Long Wing (1947)
Afterwards (1950)
Days of Plenty (1956)

Children's:
Cockleberry Castle (1963)

Two Names For Death

E. P. Fenwick

Black Gat Books • Eureka California

TWO NAMES FOR DEATH

Published by Black Gat Books
A division of Stark House Press
1315 H Street
Eureka, CA 95501, USA
griffinskye3@sbcglobal.net
www.starkhousepress.com

TWO NAMES FOR DEATH
Originally published and copyright © 1945 by Farrar &
Rinehart, Inc., New York. Reprinted in an abridged
paperback by Crestwood Publishing, Inc., New York,
1947-48, as Prize Mystery Novels, No. 28.

ISBN-13: 978-1-951473-01-3

Text design by Mark Shepard, shepgraphics.com
Proofreading by Bill Kelly
Cover illustration by Lu Kimmel from *The Violent Hours.*

First Stark House Press/Black Gat Edition:
April 2020

Chapter One

It was very quiet, and very hot, inside the taxi. The street outside, treeless and urban as it was, at least lay open to whatever listless breeze found its way up from the bay—supposing that one should do so—and the unrelenting sunshine on pavements and façades looked alive, as if it were being constantly renewed. Which it was.

But inside the taxi the shade was a delusion, the air an accumulation of the entire morning's heat; and the leather seat back kept gluing itself with quiet persistence to Barney's damp shirt. He moved forward for the tenth time in about as many minutes, felt cloth and leather peel apart, and a momentary sensation of coolness settle between his shoulder blades. Forearms crossed on the steering wheel, he stayed leaning forward this time, and peered out at the only pleasant sight in the block—the recessed entrance to the Hotel Clyde.

You didn't need the big, pale-blue sign, dripping with painted icicles, to tell you it was "Air-Conditioned." All you had to do was walk by and let your instinct suck you in. Or, if you were Barney, you sat still a few yards away and felt that same instinct point as determinedly as a willow-switch over water.

No one had emerged from the entrance for over twenty minutes, and he wasn't surprised. Not only was it the hottest day of the summer so far, but it was Sunday; and the Hotel Clyde patrons who attended to their devotions by going to church could usually be taken care of comfortably by a couple of taxis. Evidently the percentage had fallen off this morning.

Several blocks away the bells of St. Michael's began their last warning to the tardy, and Barney reached down to switch on his motor. As he did so, a man and woman came up to the plate glass doors and stopped, apparently to settle some last point before coming out into the blazing street. Barney waited with his fingers on the ignition key.

Under a white hat brim, the woman's thin, neatly painted face was animated in speech, and she pulled on her white gloves as she talked. Everything about her said that the hotel air-conditioning was working fine: there were no wrinkles in her linen suit, her powder was undamaged, and her movements had the alertness that is possible at 75° F. Something made Barney, idly watching, put them down as connected with the amusement world. Whether it was the woman's highly finished exterior, or the man's languid good looks, he didn't know. Possibly it was just the fact that the man, otherwise perfectly groomed and tailored in dark business dress, wore no hat and kept running one hand over his heavy dark hair, as if the gesture were habitual.

He seemed impatient of his companion's long, urgent speech, whatever it was, and waited with one arm braced to swing the door open. Finally his dark eyes, wandering over the street, met Barney's. He gave the door a push, and the woman, taken by surprise, stopped talking and came out into the blast of heat that was waiting for her.

The man made a brief gesture, and Barney pulled up in front of them. She turned to the man as he held the door open and said in a hesitant, fluting voice, "At least you'll wait till I come back, Francis? Surely that isn't very much to ask, and it isn't as if—"

He said, "Get in, Lenore," and waited to close the

door after her. The fluting voice said something else, sounding subdued, and the man's answer was painfully clear. He said, "You wanted to do this your way—now go ahead!" Then he turned and walked off, past the hotel entrance, leaving his companion shut into the taxi's back seat.

There was silence in the cab until that well-tailored back had turned the corner and disappeared; then Barney asked without turning: "Where to, ma'am?"

The high voice said, "Oh! Yes, I ... Those bells, driver—do they mean it's noon?"

"When they stop, it'll be eleven."

"Oh, yes. Of course." She gave a deep sigh, and added: "I'd like to go to Four Nineteen Waterford Street. In Brookline."

Involuntarily he glanced up, catching her reflection in the mirror.

"Do you know where that is?"

He said he did, and put the taxi in gear. Before they got to the corner where the man had turned, the bells stopped, and hot silence pressed down around them. Not a sound came from the back seat. He glanced again into his rearview mirror, the next time he leaned forward to free his shirt, but she had moved out of focus.

Waterford Street was somnolent under its arching trees. In the 400 block not a soul was visible; the big, shabby houses dozed side by side, left over from a more expansive era but bearing their useless cupolas and wooden fretwork with patient dignity. One of the old structures had been freshly painted—if not that year, then the one before—and it looked blatantly white between its sober neighbors. Somewhere behind it a neglected dog was yapping fretfully.

Barney drove two houses beyond, stopped, and slid

out from under the wheel. From the open windows of 419 a piano poured forth the intricacies of a Bach fugue, and the woman hesitated with one slender leg stretched out of the cab, listening.

He waited with his hand on the hot metal of the door handle, and presently she peered up at him and smiled vaguely. She looked as though the piano inside were merely one more worry added to an already long list and might as well have been playing the C scale for the pleasure it gave her; but all she said was: "Can you come back and pick me up at six this evening, driver?"

He said he could, but her big eyes were still doubtful. Nothing is settled this easily, they seemed to say. He wouldn't agree so calmly if he meant to come back....

"You won't forget?"

"No, I'll be here at six," he said gently. "I won't forget."

She paid him then, tipped him carefully, and started up the shaded walk to the porch. When he drove off she was standing in front of the screened door, making fretful adjustment of her white gloves. The piano had stopped playing.

It was still silent when he returned that evening, a little after five-thirty. He was off duty at six, and had decided to clean up for dinner before making this last haul, so that he could eat downtown before turning in his cab. He came into the front hall quietly, and went upstairs without hearing any sounds of activity from behind the heavy velvet portieres that closed the living room archway. The voice of his fare had been flutelike and clear—the kind that carries even at conversational pitch—but no echo of it reached him now. The old house was just as usual; a little quieter, if anything.

He got nearly to the top of the stairs, half wondering what had become of his nervous lady, when the bathroom door jerked open and out she came. Her hat and jacket were off, and she was making last-minute adjustment to her elaborately dressed hair. She gave him a startled glance, let her hand drop, and said, "Oh—hello," brightly. Barney said hello less brightly and kept going as though the hall were twenty feet wide, which it was not.

"You startled me for a minute. I thought everyone was downstairs."

"They probably are. I just came in."

Two more steps would have taken him by her, but she decided just then (he could see her curiosity growing) to put one hand on his sleeve in a light, playful gesture.

"It's terribly stupid of me—I know we've met, but I can't think where?"

He looked down into the pink-and-white face of a girl of eighteen, out of which a woman's tired eyes stared hungrily, cataloguing every detail of his appearance: the open shirt collar, the tousled dark hair; without his driver's cap he looked like a boy coming in from a tennis game. She treated him as if he were, and the effect was somehow unnerving. She was not more than forty-two or three, but the masklike face made her seem timeless and even sinister, like a witch in the stolen body of a young girl. Her dark red hair, worn in long, smooth waves and curls, shone in the hall light with wig-like perfection. And yet there was nothing sinister about her, outside of her appearance. Her manner was eager, strained, a little pathetic.

"I drove you out here," Barney told her, and the hand fell from his sleeve.

"You drove ... Oh. But what—?"

"I live here," he said, smiling, "so you don't have to worry about my not being here at six."

"How nice," she answered automatically, and let him go by. As he opened his door the flutelike voice came after him again.

"Driver, I—that is, I'm afraid I won't be ready at six after all. As a matter of fact, I won't want to leave until seven, and of course I wouldn't want you to wait. Perhaps I'd better just call for another taxi when I'm ready?"

He thought about it, and then said: "No, that's all right. I'll take you. The cab has to go back downtown anyway, and I'm in no hurry."

"No, no—I wouldn't dream of making you waste a whole hour!"

"I won't waste it," he assured her, still smiling, "and there's no use in two cabs making the trip out. It's all right; I'll take you down whenever you're ready."

She said, "You're very kind," in a depressed small voice, and let him go then. He could hear her sharp heels going downstairs, very slowly, as he went into his room and shut the door.

It was not cool here, either, but it was spacious and dim and private, and he was free to take off his damp shirt and heavy shoes. The idea appealed to him more than dinner at a neighborhood restaurant, and he decided to keep to his original plan of eating downtown, slightly delayed. It was too hot for hunger, anyway.

Unbuttoning his shirt, he walked to the open window overlooking the back garden and perched on its wide sill. The air outside was still and faintly greenish, as if a storm were on its way. Not a leaf or blade of grass was moving, and he didn't blame them; he would have liked nothing better himself than complete immobility followed by a good drenching.

And yet his ex-fare had looked as fresh, as carefully artificial, as she had that morning at the door of the Hotel Clyde. She was an odd all-day visitor for the Schaffts to be having. But then, any all-day visitor would have seemed curious in that house. Or even any visitor. In the two months Barney had roomed there the doorbell had rung perhaps three evenings, and was always followed by the piping voice of one of Schafft's piano pupils. Usually the fresh little voices were audible for about three words, before being shut into the music parlor across the hall from the living room. After that would come silence, or the muffled tones of the piano.

As for old Mrs. Schafft, it occurred to Barney that he had never seen her speak to anyone but her son or her granddaughter or the maid, Marja. It seemed probable that she also conversed with Bott, Barney's boss and her other roomer, since he had been there ten years or more; but Barney had never caught her at it. Even when Bott had brought him there, the introduction had been remarkably one-sided. She had simply nodded, and let him look at her—a big, pleasant-faced woman in her seventies, wearing starched cotton print that smelled of soap and sunshine. It was not until you stopped to think of it that you realized how little she had to say. Her son was garrulous in comparison.

Or garrulous by spells, at least. Barney remembered the night the music teacher had caught him on his way in and kept him on the front porch for over an hour, expounding the criminal harmonic practices of a man named Shostakovich. Since Barney's theory of harmony was to play fifths and stick to it if you could, it was a waste of both their time, intellectually. But

Schafft's need just then had not been for a fellow musi-
cologist, but merely a fellow human being; and it was
not the flourishing career of Shostakovich that was
under discussion after all, but the abandoned one of
Theodore Schafft.

Barney, sensing this after five minutes, had gone on
perching on the porch railing and lighting one cigarette after another, out of curious sympathy for the
big, untidy man mumbling away in the shadow of the
porch swing. Since then they had gone back to their
original "Hello's" and "Good evening's," and Schafft
still looked puzzled, occasionally, at meeting this
strange young man in his house.

No, definitely not a sociable household. Not that he
minded; he was there only at night, and had his own
concerns then. But he had wondered once or twice
what the granddaughter thought of her taciturn family—whether she ever had an impulse to bring five or
six noisy young people her own age home with her,
and what would happen if she did. Nothing, probably.
The household, including Bott, appeared to revolve
around her smooth dark head and she seemed content
with it as it was. Possibly it didn't occur to her that it
might be any different. She was as sedate at seventeen
as her grandmother at seventy—at least to the eye.
What had started Barney's speculation was a Chopin
Polonaise, trickling in through his open window late
one night, and certainly not played by Schafft. Even
Barney was sure of that. He had lain there listening
to it, and to the other Chopin that followed, and had
slowly developed gooseflesh.

The next time they had met in the house he looked
at her sharply, and she looked back with dark eyes
tranquil as a child's under their strong, unchildish
brows. Barney, intending to remark on the Chopin,

let her go by in her usual shy silence, and began to be afraid that he was getting shy himself.

Unless it was the family silence that was catching. Maybe his painted lady was sitting down there now, as mute as the rest of them, waiting for seven o'clock. Or else listening to a lecture on Shostakovich versus Schafft.

He grinned, got up, and made his leisurely way over a pile of discarded clothing to gather up dressing gown and bath towel. There was plenty of time for a shower, and it would be nice to eat dinner feeling like a human being, for once. He might even shave, although it wasn't really necessary.

The storm broke while he was getting dressed again. Remembering his open taxi, he dashed downstairs in bedroom slippers, rolled the windows up, and came back indoors with the first big raindrops marking his clean shirt. His fare met him in the front hall, her fluting voice lowered.

"Perhaps we had better leave before it gets too bad."

"I'll be ready in two minutes. The cab's unlocked if you'd like to go out now."

He left her hovering indecisively in front of the velvet portieres, but when he returned, in slicker and driving cap, she was no longer there. He discovered her shut into the back of the closed taxi, dabbing at rain-spots with a white handkerchief, and was suddenly impressed with the loneliness of her visit. He had seen no one come to let her in that morning, had heard no conversation at all from downstairs, and here she was on her way back without one of the family having put in an appearance. Was it possible they didn't even know she'd been there?

She told him hesitantly to take her to a hotel on

lower Commonwealth—not the Clyde—and when he had started began to question him delicately. Had he been living with the Schaffts very long? (So at least she knew their name!) No, about two months. Perhaps he was a friend of Mr. Bottman's?

"Not really a friend. I'm one of his summer drivers. I go back to school in the fall."

Would he go on living there then? No, he lived in the dormitory. In that case, she supposed, he probably hadn't gotten to know the Schaffts very well. "They're such a reserved family." Barney agreed they were, and she went back to her own thoughts, apparently satisfied. Now what was that for, he wondered—la politesse, or information?

When they got to the hotel—a small, conservative one—the rain was coming down in sheets, and thunder cracked overhead periodically. She hesitated on the edge of her seat, measuring the distance to safety, and murmured: "I just wanted to run in for a minute. Perhaps if we wait, it will stop a little."

"Can I do your errand for you?"

"No, no," she said quickly. "Thank you."

They waited in silence for five minutes, and then an elderly bellhop with an umbrella came out to take her in. She was gone an incredibly short time before the bellhop, looking disgruntled, brought her back and shut her up in the taxi again. She handed him some money in silence, and said "Hotel Clyde" to Barney, with all the lilt gone out of her voice. She didn't say a word on the trip there.

When Barney returned to the house on Waterford Street, a little before nine, the rain had stopped and the air was fresh and cool. There was a light on in the Schaffts' living room, and he could see the girl seated at the huge piano placed near the window. She was not playing but sat there immobile, her hands in her lap, as though she were wondering what to play.

For the rest of the evening, half-unconsciously, he was waiting for that contemplated music to begin. It never did; but just as he was dropping off to sleep he heard Schafft's heavy hands strike the first slow chords of a Beethoven Sonata, and then stop. That was all the music there was, that evening.

Chapter Two

The impersonal efficiency of a large hotel is capable of absorbing a great deal of irregular activity without disturbing its patrons in the least. It is too much to expect that several thousand assorted persons should be gathered together under one roof every night without a few of them, at least, presenting some sort of peculiarity; but so long as the peculiarities are quiet ones and confined to the space rented for them, no one is apt to object. And in any case, a guest's behavior is a matter between himself and the management, and the management most earnestly wishes to keep it that way, with a tacit motto of "Sleep, and let sleep."

The average guest has no quarrel with this discreet policy, and is accustomed to regard any hotel management as a combination whipping boy and supreme authority, depending on his mood of the moment. Whatever happens, it is the management's problem, and the management is expected to deal with it.

Even the arrival of a large number of purposeful men, some in police uniform and some not, and a congestion of scout cars and police sedans at the door, cannot really disrupt the routine of a large hotel. The lobby bystanders are impressed, a little nervous, certainly curious; but the elevator doors close implacably on the grim visitors, the desk clerks know nothing, and the bellboys' faces are blank. There is nothing to do but drift away, and wait for the next edition of the papers.

Before noon one Monday in August, this was what took place at the Hotel Clyde. Perhaps two per cent of the guests were aware of it: those in the lobby, and those whose rooms were on the sixth floor, whose corridors were guarded by uncommunicative, uniformed police. The door of 617 was closed like any other door; whatever was wrong was shut behind its blank surface, and only the men on guard before it distinguished it from its neighbors.

But the room itself was a hotel manager's nightmare. The chairs, the furniture tops, and most of the floor space were crowded with men and purposeful equipment; the air was already thick, and the bed was unmade and smeared with blood. On it lay the nightgown-clad body of a woman, the head and one arm dangling over the edge; and the rug beneath the limp hand was dark with blood. Dark red hair hung down to conceal the face, and swayed slightly when the bed was touched.

The police photographer said angrily, when this happened, "Jeez, will you quit bouncing her?" and went on making exposures until the woman had been photographed from every angle. When he was satisfied he said, "Okay, doc, she's all yours"; and the man from the Medical Examiner's office came up to the bedside.

The limp arm was not quite as limp as it appeared, but it yielded to the doctor's careful maneuvering. Lieutenant Eggart of the Homicide Squad, who had been watching for this, turned away and leaned over the small hotel desk, with its customary lamp, blotter, and stationery rack. Two sheets of the hotel notepaper lay on the blotter, one half covering the other, as if the writer had finished one page and taken a fresh one. The bottom sheet was covered with writing, and the second sheet had only a line and a half across the top.

Leaning down, and not touching the paper, Eggart saw written in a woman's loose, round hand: "... mustn't think badly of me for having made it ." That was all; no signature. He straightened up and said, "Hey, Harry—make a couple of prints of this, a will you? Just the top of the desk."

He waited while this was done; and then while the fingerprint expert was at work on the nearly blank sheet he pulled the other one free with a match-tip and leaned over it once more.

"My dear," the letter began. "I hoped we would have another chance to talk, because I want you to understand I didn't plan for things to turn out this way—I never dreamed they would. God knows you deserve better of life and of me. But I have learned at last not to fight against destiny. Sometimes it takes more courage not to fight, but that's a kind of courage you only learn after years of sorrow and trial. Believe me, I've known both—this wasn't an easy decision to make, and you ..."

The Lieutenant came to the end of the page, his expression blank, and then said only: "Mahaney, do you have to breathe down my neck?" His sergeant, a slower reader, made absent apology and moved into the lieutenant's vacated place. Eggart crossed the room to where the hotel manager was standing, near the door, nibbling his cuticles.

"If you wouldn't mind waiting in your office, Mr. Corby, I'd like to talk to you when we're finished here.

You might get hold of her registration slip, and any other information you'd have about her."

"Yes, of course, Lieutenant. The slip is already available, but I'm afraid there's really nothing—"

"I'll go over it with you later, then," said Eggart firmly, and opened the door. The manager, who was not used to having his troubles handled for him, backed out reluctantly.

"The freight elevator—"

"We'll be ready for it in fifteen minutes or so." He shut the door, and went over to the bed. The doctor said without turning:

"All I can tell you now is that she slit her wrists sometime after midnight and died before five this morning. She's had some kind of sleeping stuff, but you'll have to wait for the report on that. As far as I'm concerned you can pack her up."

"This what she used?" Eggart asked, indicating a safety-razor blade which had been clamped into a patented metal holder about three inches long. The question seemed superfluous, since the blade and holder were both badly stained with blood, but the doctor nodded quietly.

"No reason why not. I've got one of those blade-holders myself, at home. Use it for mounting pictures—cutting the mat, you know. They're handy little things, but they make a wicked weapon. Never seen deeper wrist wounds—right down to the bone."

"Both wrists?" Eggart asked. The doctor looked at him sharply.

"Just alike. I'll get a report to you soon as I can."

With the departure of the doctor, the woman's body, and several of the uniformed men, the room lost some of its chaotic aspect. The fingerprint man was still busily at work, however, and Eggart came to stand beside him.

"How's it going?"

"Okay. The razor-dingus is hopeless—you can't get prints on that much fresh blood, you know; just smears. When it congeals, you got nothing. Her prints are on the letter and the pen, and the suitcase metal, and everything else you'd expect, but there's a couple of funny things."

"Like what?"

"Well, she had a visitor, for one thing. A man. Got a whole set of his prints off that glass on the bureau, and some on one of the straight chairs, and the door. But the glass by the bed hasn't got a print on it—hers, or anybody's."

Eggart said "Yeah?" softly, and glanced at the bed-side table. The glass that stood there still held about a quarter of an inch of what appeared to be water. "We'll take that along with us, Mahaney," he said to the sergeant, who was squatting in front of an open dressing case. "The stuff, I mean—not the glass. See if you can get hold of a little bottle downstairs, will you? Only make sure it's clean—rinsed out in boiling water."

The sergeant transmitted this order through the partially opened door and then came back to join Eggart beside the bed. The lieutenant was examining the crumpled bedclothes, which had been turned down to free the body for examination and removal. Apparently the woman had slept under a sheet only; the spread had been neatly folded back, as if by the woman herself, and the lightweight blanket removed and placed on a chair, folded. But the top sheet was badly stained and rumpled. Eggart straightened it out carefully and examined the long gashes thus revealed.

"Looks like she carved the sheet up too, don't it?" the sergeant remarked.

"I'd say those were the same cuts that went through to her wrists, from the blood around them," said Eggart thoughtfully.

"Could be. That's a funny way to do. You'd think she'd take her arms out from under the sheet first wouldn't you? Unless maybe she didn't want to see what she was doing."

"She went to a lot of trouble to keep from seeing," Eggart remarked. "That razor had to change hands, to cut both wrists, and the sheet would make it pretty complicated." They stood regarding the bed for some time in silence, and then Eggart added: "Well, let's take the sheet along too. You can start packing up Mahaney; we'll look her things over down at head-quarters. I'll meet you down in the manager's office."

The manager, standing restlessly in the middle of his own office, came forward as Eggart was ushered in the door and made an attempt to smile.

"I'm afraid I haven't anything for you, Lieutenant. I've checked on her calls, as far as I can, but there's nothing except one local outgoing call. We've no record of the number."

"That's too bad," said Eggart, "but it looks like the real job is going to be a general check-up with your staff. My fingerprint man tells me she had a man with her, up there. I'd like to find out if anyone noticed him."

"A man?" The manager's tentative smile vanished, and after a moment he returned to his desk as though it were a kind of refuge. "She was registered alone. I have the slip here—'Mrs. Lenore Bellane, New York.' Are you sure the fingerprints are—recent ones?"

"They are if you wash your glasses between cus-

tomers," Eggart smiled, and examined the printed
form on which the dead woman had registered. The
date, name and home address had been filled in in
the same round hand as the letter he had recently
read; and someone else had marked the number "617"
on it. "I'll take this along, Mr. Corby. I see she registered
Saturday—do you know what time?"

"Yes, I have it here. Just a moment ... about nine-
thirty at night." He looked at the police officer with
anxious, wary eyes. "This check-up of the staff—that's
going to be a pretty long job, you realize. Of course
you're welcome to use my office as long as you need
it."

"We'll keep it as quiet as we can," Eggart told him,
aware of the other's meaning. "I'll leave a couple of
men here, and you can arrange things any way you
want them—just so they get a chance to contact every
likely employee. Bellboys, chambermaids, bartenders,
and so on."

Corby said he understood, but looked depressed as
Mahaney and two uniformed men appeared. Eggart
introduced them, gave them their instructions, and
then took Mahaney back to headquarters with him.
Here the dead woman's belongings were waiting to
be examined: a dressing case, neatly packed by Mahaney, and a white plastic handbag.

She had evidently been planning on a short stay.
Besides her lingerie and cosmetics, which were expensive and in good condition, there was only the
linen suit, taken from its hanger, and one dark dress.
Her handbag held compact, comb, mirror, a key case
with two Yale keys and three smaller ones, cigarette
case and lighter, and a leather billfold containing thirty
dollars in cash, a return ticket to New York, a social
security card in the name of Lenore Bellane, and a

snapshot of a young girl.

This last was the only personal thing she had had with her, so far as Eggart could discover, and he put it aside until the report from New York came in.

Long before he looked for them, and only a short while after he had left the hotel, he got his first results from the employee check-up. One of the dining room waiters had served breakfast on Sunday to Lenore Bellane and a man; he not only remembered them, but proved it by describing the woman in detail.

Brought down to headquarters, he gave his name as John Zerka and said the two of them had occupied one of his tables around nine, when he wasn't too busy to pay attention to them.

"Sure, I saw her good. Thin, and not real young, but nice-looking. She had red hair, and some kind of white dress. Isn't that her? One reason I remember is that she was the only one that had breakfast—the guy said he'd had his, and he didn't look like it agreed with him."

He described the "guy" with sober care: a tall fellow, close to fifty, maybe, but looked young for his age. Had a good figure, and was a "dresser"; looked kind of like an ex-movie star, though he didn't know which one. Close up he didn't look so healthy, but still he was a good-looker, the kind women went for. Kind of pale, with dark eyes and heavy dark eyebrows, and lot of black hair without a thread of grey in it. Mr. Zerka, whose own dark head had a faint reddish tint in the light, gave his opinion that the black hair was "natural," and said it was funny the way some people didn't turn till real late in life.

He said Mrs. Bellane had eaten a light breakfast while her companion drank coffee and looked on; the lady did most of the talking, and Zerka thought she

was trying to persuade the man into something—
what, he didn't know. The man himself hadn't had
much to say, and about nine-thirty he paid the bill
and took the woman away. Zerka didn't know where
they went from there.

Eggart, pleased, translated the description of Mrs.
Bellane's companion into official language and gave
it out. He was more and more grateful for it as the
day went on, and other leads came to nothing. Information from New York was meager: the woman lived
alone on West Twelfth Street in a one-room efficiency;
she had no discoverable family, no intimates among
the neighbors, traveled a lot (on business, the caretaker thought), and seemed to have a good, steady income. There was no reference to the young girl of the
snapshot.

The chemist's report on the liquid in the bedside
glass was equally flat; it was the remains of a sedative.
The dose was strong, but not in the least dangerous; a
normal dose for someone who habitually took help in
sleeping.

Finally, to wind up the day, Dr. Marshall of the M.
E.'s office dropped in to see Eggart and said at once
with great cheer:

"Well, I think you've got yourself a murder this time,
Eggart."

"How do you figure it?"

"The wounds, mainly. You'll get it in the report, but
this is the ABC of it. When you want to cut your wrist
open"—he demonstrated on his own—"you get your
razor, or whatever it is, in your right hand and you
bring it across your left wrist like this—from the outside in. You may botch it up a little, till you get going,
but the entrance is on the outside of the wrist, and
the direction of the cut is toward you. Same thing

with the other wrist, in reverse: you start on the side away from you, and pull in. That's where you get your leverage; it's instinctive.

"But these wounds both go from right to left, which means she would have had to pull the razor across one wrist and push it across the other. Besides, the incision slant is away from her hand instead of towards it, which would mean that the poor lady had her razor in a mighty awkward grip. Another thing is the depth of the wounds. A good, strong hand made them, and made them both just alike. If the woman had done her own carving, she might have got the left wrist that deep, but the right one would have come out lighter and not so neat, because the left hand wasn't functioning as well as the right had been. Then, too, the cuts are too clean. Too businesslike. I've seen pretty many, but none that didn't have a few unnecessary nicks before the real wound. She didn't."

"But why didn't she put up any fight?" Eggart asked. "There wasn't a bruise or a mark on her, and yet she didn't have anything but a regular sleeping dose, according to the chemist's report. Did you look for head bruises?"

"I did, and there isn't a sign of one. But you better tell your chemist to look again. If the dose she had wasn't out of the ordinary for her, she must have had a tolerance I've never heard of before. She'd had enough to knock a horse out."

"Not out of the glass by her bed."

"Well, that's your problem," said Dr. Marshall generously, and made for the door. "Just thought you'd like to hear the good news without waiting for the report."

Eggart thanked him as gravely as though he really had brought pleasant news, and went on with his work. One elevator boy remembered taking Mrs. Bellane and her friend upstairs sometime Sunday morning, but had only a hazy idea of their appearance. Nobody remembered them coming down, or had seen them during the rest of the day or evening, either together or apart. Either Mr. John Zerka was the only Clyde employee with his eyes peeled, or Mrs. Bellane and friend had been using back entrances.

And that could be, too, Eggart thought, getting up to put his hat on and call it a day.

Chapter Three

A little after nine the following morning Mr. Edward J. Bottman, owner and proprietor of the Bottman Taxi Company, pushed open the swinging gate that divided his private domain from the more public part of his office, and went at once to hang his coat on the communal tree. There was only one other person in the large, shabby room from which Mr. Bottman directed his fleet's activities—a restless boy named Hookey, who watched his employer's entrance with sharp eyes, but said nothing.

Mr. Bottman had nothing to say either; but presently he turned, flipped a fifty-cent piece across the barrier, and waited to see it land. Hookey, to whom this was routine but pleasant duty, caught the coin skillfully and went out, whistling, after two mugs of coffee and whatever else should catch his fancy. Mr. Bottman meanwhile settled down to wait behind his own desk, with his large feet on the morning mail, and quietly released most of his buttons from active duty.

The weather was still cool and fresh from Sunday's storm, but Mr. Bottman was neither. A big, heavy-bodied man who lived chiefly on plenty of steaks, French-fries, and beer, he was not comfortable with the temperature above seventy; but he bore his summer discomfort stoically, as he bore everything else. His little gray eyes were still alert and shrewd in his flaming red face, and his traplike long mouth lost none of its controlled tightness under the heat's pressure. If his temper got somewhat shorter as the summer grew long, it too was under control. Even Hookey would admit that you had to "ask for it" before you got it—but then you really got it.

As a matter of general policy, no one usually disturbed Mr. Bottman—never known as anything but "Bott"—until he had had his morning coffee, fished the mail out from under his feet, and done a little growling over it. But this morning, before Hookey had even returned, the outer door swung open and a dark, wiry young man in the Bottman driver's cap came in.

He got an instant hard stare from behind the desk, said "good morning" to it, and watched the traplike mouth relax. It was impossible not to know that Bott was partial to his "college boys." He employed them whenever he could during the summer, excused their mistakes, and infuriated his older drivers by pointing out the benefits of education whenever one of them turned in an unblemished cab and a good day's receipts. The "college boys" found themselves walking a tightrope between Bott's blanket approval and the other drivers' secret hostility, and most of them fell off before a month was out. But a few stuck, a few who desperately needed the money, or liked a good fight, or somehow managed to keep out of the other drivers' bad graces.

The dark young man was one of these survivors, and the last of that year's crop. Now in his second summer as a Bottman driver, he had managed to achieve tolerance and even one friend among the other men—and to become, as he was sometimes uncomfortably aware, a genuine protégé of his employer.

"Well, doctor," said Bott now. "How's the professor this morning?" He took his feet down as he spoke, and stretched out a large hand.

"All right, thanks."

"Sit down. What's on your mind?"

"You haven't had the police around this morning, have you?"

The little grey eyes blinked, and became watchful. "I have not. You been passing red lights, young Barney?"

"No, but I think they're looking for me just the same. I had a fare they're interested in."

"Did you," said Bott, and grinned with relief. "Well, you better go over to the precinct station and report. They may take you down to headquarters and lose you half a day's take, but we can't help that. Who is it?"

Barney shook his head, and put a folded newspaper under the other's eyes. "That's all I know about it. The Hotel Clyde piece."

Bott leaned forward, bent his red face over the paper, and read solemnly, "'Mystery Man Sought in Hotel Death.' That one?"

"Yes."

"And you picked up the Mystery Man, eh?"

"I think so. Go ahead and read it, Bott."

An edge of sharpness in Barney's voice made the older man glance at him before he went back to the paper. He read aloud, slowly, following his heavy finger across the lines.

"'Police are today seeking to trace a man known to

be the companion of the woman who died last Sunday night in her room at the Hotel Clyde. According to evidence of hotel employees, the man, who was not a guest at the hotel, was seen breakfasting with the dead woman Sunday morning, and fingerprint evidence indicated that he had also visited her in her room only a short time before she was found dead of deep slashes in both wrists.' My!" said Bott, looking up.

"Go on, Bott."

"The woman, registered as a Mrs. ... a Mrs. Lenore Bellane ..." The finger lost its direction and slid from the paper. After a minute Bott looked up again and this time his heavy face had lost much of its color.

"You do know her?"

The little grey eyes got Barney's face in their focus, with difficulty.

"Know her? Know Lenore? My God, she ... But Sunday night! It says here she was dead Sunday night—"

"They found her yesterday morning. It was in last night's paper, name and all. You didn't see it?"

"In last night's paper?"

"I looked it up this morning, after I saw this. About ten lines, in with the local news. It carried her name."

Bott shook his head, and after a moment pushed the paper across the desk. "Read it to me, Barney. Read me the rest of it."

Barney picked up the paper and went on, aloud: "'The woman, registered as a Mrs. Lenore Bellane of New York and a guest at the hotel since the preceding Saturday night, was discovered by a hotel employee late Monday morning, lying in bed with both wrists deeply cut and a razor on the floor beside her. Medical examination disclosed that she had died sometime during the previous night. Fingerprints found in Mrs.

Bellane's room indicated that she had not been alone on the day of her death, and this was later borne out by evidence of John Zerka, waiter in the hotel restaurant, and an elevator attendant who reported taking the dead woman and her companion upstairs sometime before noon Sunday. Both describe the man as tall, slender, and in his late forties, with heavy dark hair and eyebrows and pale complexion. He was dressed in a dark suit and probably wore no hat. Police are seeking to discover a taxi driver who may have picked him up Sunday night or Monday morning early, in the vicinity of the hotel.'"

Hookey, laden walked into the ensuing silence. With a curious glance at the two men he set a mug of black coffee, two large sweet rolls and some change in front of the silent Bott, who looked at them as if they were elements of nightmare and said angrily, "What's this?"

"What d'you think it is?" said Hookey, outraged "Poison iodine an' horse manure, o' course! That's what you told me to get, ain't it?"

Bott rubbed his face impatiently and got up.

"Come on, Barney. Let's get started. I'll go with you. Hook, you tell Sadie I've gone out, and the both of you stay here till I get back, whenever it is. Understand?"

"Sure," said Hookey, his eyes quick between Barney and the untouched coffee. "Sure, Bott. Go ahead."

Bott took down his crumpled jacket once more, mashed it under his arm, and followed Barney out to his waiting taxi. He said nothing as they got under way, and Barney kept his own curiosity quiet. As they turned the corner Bott touched his arm.

"Not that way. We'll take this straight to headquarters."

"Okay."

Bott turned suddenly, so that his eyes were on Bar-

ney. "You couldn't have picked him up Sunday night.
You weren't on duty."

"I didn't. It was Sunday morning, about eleven."

"Did you see her?"

"She was with him. He put her in the taxi and
walked away. I took her out to the Schaffts'."

"Oh, Christ," said Bott harshly, and slid down in his
seat. "Well, it can't be helped. That's why you came to
me first, huh? It's all right, Barney. You did right. But
God knows what *I* can do about it."

"What's it all about, Bott?"

"Edith," he said violently. "That's what it'll *be* about.
The sweetest, best kid in the world. A real little lady—
you know what she's like, Barney! You've seen her,
and heard her play on the piano just like the little angel she is. A girl like Edith, mixed up in a mess like
this! It'll ruin her life, that's what it'll do. Ruin her
life!"

"Why should she get mixed up in it? You live there
and so do I, and I don't think either one of us will he
sleeping in jail tonight."

"You don't understand, son. Lenore was Edith's
mother. Lenore Bellane Schafft was her right name,
only I guess Schafft wasn't toney enough for her. God
rest her soul—poor Lenore! She wasn't much good,
but I never thought she'd end up this way."

"Schafft was her husband?"

"That's right. You see what a mess it'll be, Barney."

"It's not good, certainly. Sorry, Bott. I know they're
friends of yours."

A violent clutch at his arm sent the wheel momentarily out of his grasp, and the car out of its course.
He recovered, glanced sideways, and discovered Bott
on the edge of his seat, beating on the dashboard.

"Stop the car, Barney! What's the matter with me? I

can't go down there with you! Why, they don't know a thing about this—and me, the only friend they got in the world, hot-footing it down to the police! I got to tell them, Barney—I got to get out there and find Edith myself, before them cops break it to her. Pull over here to the side a minute."

Barney obeyed, and stopped Bott with a hand on his arm as he was pushing his big body out the half-open door.

"Wait a minute. You're sure they don't know already, Bott? Don't any of them read the papers?"

The little grey eyes met his, sharp and hostile.

"What d'you mean by that, son? If they knew, they'd have done something about it, wouldn't they?"

"I didn't say they wouldn't." Curiosity pricked at his mind but he put it down, under Bott's tragic, belligerent stare. "How do you know they haven't done something about it already? Did you see any of them before you left?"

"I saw Marthe," said Bott slowly. "She didn't know. And if they heard about it since, they would have called me."

"Marthe? That's old Mrs. Schafft?"

Bott nodded, and pulled his arm free.

"Go ahead, Barney. I'll get out here. We're wasting time."

"You'll waste more time starting out this way, Bott. Take the cab, and let me walk it. We're pretty close, and it'll give you more time, if that's what you want."

"All right. Good boy. You ask for Lieutenant Eggart and tell him I sent you—he knows me."

Barney slid out onto the sidewalk, shut his employer in the taxi, and watched it pull away, smooth and fast. Then, feeling incomplete in his driver's cap, with nothing to drive, he set off through the morning crowd toward police headquarters.

He wasn't sorry he had talked to Bott first, whether this preliminary warning was ethical or not—and he didn't see why not. But what he had learned didn't clear up anything; it only made the whole situation more fantastic. It was easier to think of his flute-voiced fare with her wrists slashed, in the Hotel Clyde, than to imagine her as Schafft's wife, and the girl's mother. But apparently she was both women. It seemed odd there should be no link between the two except a taxi driver.

He wasn't pleased to be that particular taxi driver, either. He supposed that police investigation would have turned up other links sooner or later between Mrs. Schafft of Brookline and the anonymous Lenore Bellane of New York, connected with no one but a vanished "Mystery Man." But what if it hadn't? Was it possible for a woman to die spectacularly in the same city with her family, and neither that family nor the police to be aware of the connection?

No matter how careless the family was about news-paper reading, no matter how little identification the woman herself might carry, weren't there a hundred other ways the truth might come out? The Schaffts had lived there for a long while. You'd think at least one of the neighbors would recognize the maiden name of Schafft's wife. Yet, remembering that silent house in Brookline, and the telephone and doorbell that never rang, Barney wasn't so sure. The woman could have died in the house itself, probably, without the neighbors on either side being aware of it.

The idea, crossing his mind carelessly, left a feeling of distaste in its wake. For while she clearly had not died in the Schaffts' house, she hadn't missed doing so by many hours. It must have been in her mind when he had met her in the upstairs hall that evening, and he had seen nothing but an overpainted, over-mannered, rather pitiful woman grappling with minor embarrassments. *"I know we've met ..."*

We have indeed, he thought grimly. Right outside the Hotel Clyde, when you were alive, and the Mystery Man was with you. For what good it does any of us, Mrs. Bellane-Schafft, I guess I remember, all right.

Chapter Four

Lieutenant Eggart of the Homicide Squad could have passed for the Mystery Man himself, if he had been seven or eight years older. Tall, thin, with heavy black hair and eyebrows and the clear, pale skin of the "Black Irish," he nevertheless bore little other resemblance to Lenore Bellane's vanished companion. His manner was deliberate rather than languid, and he looked far more healthy and alert than the other, but the main characteristics would have fitted either one—and probably a lot of other men in the city as well.

It occurred to Barney that a lot of cockeyed reports must come in from a description as vague as the Mystery Man's—and that it would be no fun sorting them out. A clear lack of enthusiasm in Eggart's manner made him suspect there had already been some time-wasters on this case.

"So you picked him up, did you? One of Bott's drivers? What's your name?"

"Chance. Barnard Chance."

"You'll be one of them college boys of his," observed a gloomy-looking sergeant sitting on the window sill. "I can tell from the look of you."

Eggart said impatiently, "I don't care if you're the President of Harvard, so long as you had your taxi outside the Clyde Sunday night. Did you?"

"No. It was earlier than that. I picked him up about eleven that morning."

"And ain't that lovely," said the sergeant.

Eggart, who had started to put down his pencil, glanced coldly at the sergeant and said with restraint: "What good is Sunday morning? She was alive then."

"I know. She was with him."

"Was she. How do you know it was she? There haven't been any pictures."

"I don't. But he answers your description, and he called her Lenore."

"What did she look like?"

"Medium height, thin, somewhere in her forties. A lot of make-up, and dark red hair. She had on a white suit and hat and gloves."

"You look your customers over, don't you? Where'd you take them?"

"I didn't take him anywhere. He put her in the car and walked away."

"Away where?"

"Just around the corner—not back into the hotel."

"And then what?"

"Then she gave me an address, and I took her there. Out in Brookline."

"Brookline ? A private home ? Do you remember where it was?"

"Yes. Four Nineteen Waterford Street."

Eggart wrote it down. "You're sure that's the address? Pretty good memory, haven't you?"

"I live there."

This time the pencil did go down, but it was the sergeant who said blankly: "Hey, what is this? You mean you took her to your own house?"

"The house where I room. She told me to come back for her at six, and I did, but she wasn't ready to leave. We didn't start till the storm broke—about six-thirty, I guess. I took her to a hotel over on Commonwealth—the Standish. She went in for a couple of minutes, came right out, and went back to the Clyde. That was the last I saw of her."

"And of him?"

"Yes."

"You hadn't ever seen her before? Didn't know who she was?"

"No. I just thought she was a friend of the people I room with."

The lieutenant stared at him a minute longer, then lifted a pack of cigarettes from the desk top, shook one out, and lit it.

"Who are these people you room with?"

"A family named Schafft. A man about fifty, his mother, and his daughter. Bott rooms there too."

"Bott does? Have you talked to him about this?"

"Yes, this morning."

"Does he know her?"

"He says so."

"Not to us, he ain't," said the sergeant.

Eggart said, "Mahaney," and then: "Let's get this straight, Chance. You didn't have any idea your fare was Mrs. Bellane until you read the papers this morning? You didn't know her name before then?"

"No."

"Then you told Bott your story, and he admitted it was Mrs. Bellane?"

"He recognized the name, and sent me down here to you."

"*Sent* you here? Where's he?"

"I don't know," said Barney, feeling that this was technically true.

"Why didn't he come with you, if he knows this woman?"

"You'll have to ask him, Lieutenant."

"I will, thanks. Mahaney, send someone over to pick Bott up and bring him back here." When the sergeant left the room he said slowly, with his eyes on Barney, "You think this woman was out there to see Bott, Sunday?"

"No, I don't think she was. I gathered from what he said that it was the Schaffts she'd gone out to see."

"You gathered? From what? What did he say, exactly?"

"He didn't say anything very exactly, Lieutenant. He was more than half talking to himself. You can get the straight of it better from him, or from the Schaffts maybe. All I know is that I picked the man up Sunday morning—"

"Nuts," said Eggart. "What are you so cagey about? What was it Bott said?"

"Nothing he wouldn't say to you. I'm not cagey; I just don't like turning in other people's evidence for them when they're around to do it better for themselves. Besides, I don't know what this is all about any more than you do. There's no use in my sitting here and mixing us both up."

Unexpectedly, the lieutenant's eyes crinkled. "You wouldn't be a law student, would you?"

Barney said no, engineering; and Eggart nodded. He wrote rapidly on the paper in front of him for a few seconds, stuffed it in his pocket, and flipped a key on the intercommunication box beside him. "Get a car around front for me, will you? And tell Cooney I'm out on the Bellane case—back before noon, or I'll call in.

Come on," he added to Barney. "We'll play this your way for a while. But you'll sit in."

Waterford Street was indifferent to the advent of Lieutenant Eggart, his sergeant, and his neatly lettered sedan. No curtains moved, and a woman busy with a flowerbed next door to 419 looked at them briefly and then turned back to the moist earth under her fingers. Barney, who had ridden out in the front seat beside Eggart, the driver, got out first and held the door. Eggart emerged slowly, his dark eyes looking over the big white house. Mahaney grunted his way out of the back of the car and stood where he landed. He said:

"I ain't pushing no doorbells round here. This is the kid's party, it's on him. Go ahead, Mr. Chance."

Barney moved up the walk, Eggart beside him, the sergeant in the rear. Luckily, Barney's missing cab had caused no remark; outside headquarters, in reply to Eggart's "Where's your cab?" he had said only that it was all right, and that had sufficed. But there had been little talk during the drive, and Barney was still aware of being regarded as more of a bird-in-the-hand than an independent witness. The taxi was nowhere to be seen; he tried not to wonder about it.

At the door, Eggart motioned Barney aside and rang. They waited, in hot silence, for a long while. Just as Eggart lifted his hand again the knob turned and the old door moved inward quietly until it was half open. Mrs. Marthe Schafft stood in the opening; from behind her the muffled notes of a piano drifted out. She said nothing; her expression was serious, pleasant, a little remote. Her old eyes moved impartially from one to the other of them.

Lieutenant Eggart took off his hat. "Good morning—I'm Lieutenant Eggart from police headquarters. Sorry to bother you, but we're looking for information about a Mrs. Lenore Bellane." He pronounced it "Bell- ne," carefully. Mrs. Schafft said:

"There is no one here by that name, Lieutenant." It was the longest sentence Barney had heard her produce, and she did it slowly.

"We have information that she was a visitor here last Sunday."

"I do not know anyone by that name."

There was a short silence. Just as Barney opened his mouth the Lieutenant said, indicating him: "Do you know this young man?"

Mrs. Schafft's eyes met his, deepset and untroubled. Then she nodded, once. "He is our roomer." She said to Barney, without sternness. "Are you in trouble?"

"I don't think so, Mrs. Schafft. Perhaps you'd recognize the name if it were pronounced 'Bel-uh-nee'?" This was Bott's pronunciation. It seemed to have no effect on her, except that after another pause she nodded once again.

"I know the name. I do not know a Mrs. Lenore Bellane."

"Perhaps—"

Eggart cut in. "Is your son here, Mrs. Schafft? I'd like to talk to him."

"He is engaged, Lieutenant."

"Will you ask him if he'll see me for a minute?"

"I cannot interrupt him now."

The sergeant made a smothered sound from the background. Eggart said over it, "We'll wait, if you don't mind."

She stood there, unresponsive, until Eggart made a slight forward movement. Then she took two deliberate steps out of their way, waited until they had entered the cool, dark-paneled hall, and shut the door quietly behind them. The piano became suddenly very loud inside the house; inexpert fingers were staggering through a Schubert three-finger arrangement. Mrs. Schafft said, "Sit down, please," and waited until they had done so, in a row, on a built-in bench at one side of the hall. Then she left them without another word.

The sergeant grunted, and peered across Eggart to Barney. "You got any more hot tips, Mr. Chance?"

"No. Would you rather wait upstairs in my room?"

"This is all right," Eggart answered briefly.

It wasn't. The tortured Schubert went on and on, Mrs. Schafft remained invisible, and the uncovered bench got harder and more crowded with every minute.

After a while Barney got up.

"All right if I run upstairs a minute?"

"I'll come with you. Mahaney, you wait here."

They went up side by side, in silence. Barney pushed open the door of his room, let the lieutenant in, and went across the hall to the bathroom. When he came back Eggart was sitting on the window sill, smoking. The door stood open. He left it that way, sat down on the bed, and lit one of his own cigarettes.

Eggart said, expressionlessly, "Maybe you guessed wrong, Chance."

"I haven't done any guessing, Lieutenant. I brought a woman here Sunday, from the Hotel Clyde—that's all I know. You might ask her who it was."

"Don't worry. I'll get around to everything. If there's anything in this, we'll find it. If there isn't, you'll wish there was."

Barney made no reply. Presently Eggart stubbed out his cigarette and rose. "Is there a phone around?"

"On the landing."

"Come on. We'll go back down."

On the landing Eggart motioned him to go past, and Barney rejoined the glowering Mahaney in the downstairs hall. Above them the lieutenant's low voice was audible through the disjointed piano notes.

"Bottman shown up? Well, keep on trying. Anything else? Okay—that's all."

As he replaced the receiver a car drew up before the house, brakes squealing. Barney started for the door, and the sergeant's hard fingers bit into his arm.

"Take it easy, little man. Hey, Lieutenant!"

"Okay. Just stay where you are."

The car door slammed, and there was a confused sound of footsteps coming up the walk. They could see nothing through the only outlet—beveled glass set high in the old door; but when the door itself opened, the three of them were standing there, waiting.

They must have had a menacing look, Barney realized, looming up in the dim space. The girl who entered shrank back with a faint exclamation, and Bott's red face appeared over her shoulder, staring fiercely. He said at once, "It's all right, honey. Only Barney, and some friends of mine. You go on upstairs like a good girl, and I'll send your granny to you."

She didn't move, except that her eyes went from Barney to Eggart to Mahaney, and stopped there, on his uniform. The strong brows made a line over her clear dark eyes—an oddly heavy line in that otherwise defenseless face. She said to Mahaney:

"You're a policeman—why are you here? Is it something about my mother? Is it?"

Mahaney went back a step, and stammered, "Well, now, young lady—well, now, I—"

"Honey, listen to your old Bott—"

She cried out suddenly, "Oh, Bott, Bott! I knew you weren't telling me everything! You mean to be kind, but it's not kind—what is it? What is it?"

"Wait a minute, Bott," Eggart interrupted. "You're Miss Schafft? My name is Eggart, from police headquarters. If you don't mind, we'd like to talk to Mr. Bottman first; then I'll be glad to tell you anything I can. All right?"

It wasn't all right. They could see her apprehension deepen with every word he said, but her nature was clearly an obedient one, and Eggart's quiet voice had the effect he wanted. After one long stare at him she turned quickly away and ran upstairs. Bott watched her go, and Eggart watched him.

As soon as the girl was out of earshot, the lieutenant said sharply: "All right, Bott. Let's have it. Everything you know about this Bellane woman. And I mean everything!"

Chapter Five

A door closed over their heads, and Bott's belligerence collapsed. He looked at the three of them, nodded, and turned toward the living room portieres, which were close-drawn.

"Sure; glad to. We better go in here. Where is everybody?"

"We'd like to know that ourselves," said Mahaney tartly. "Bott, this here driver of yours—"

He stopped. The door opposite the portieres, from behind which the piano lesson had been audible, was suddenly pulled open. A tall, heavily built man of middle age and untidy appearance came out, shut the door at his back, and stood regarding them. His greying hair and moustache, both long and badly kept, and his equally heavy eyebrows, gave his head an oversized appearance, even on that large body. But the features of the face were unexpectedly fine and clear-cut. He said in a deep voice, to none of them in particular:

"Was that Edith? What's she doing home from the Conservatory? Is anything wrong?"

"Mr. Schafft?" The big man looked Eggart over carefully before saying "Yes." "Lieutenant Eggart, from police headquarters. We're looking for information about a Mrs. Lenore Bellane."

Bott, with a muttered "Back in a minute," walked between them toward the back of the house; Mahaney moved after him, and they both disappeared from view. Schafft, his eyes puzzled, repeated: "From the police? What kind of information?"

"You know her?"

A slight, bitter smile tipped the man's lips, and was gone.

"Certainly I know her. Since you're here at all, you're probably aware that she is my wife, in spite of her carelessness about names. Come in, please. I hope nothing is wrong?" He caught sight of Barney in the background, hesitated, and said, "Yes, Mr. Hm?"

"Sorry, Mr. Schafft. Do you want me any longer, Lieutenant?"

"I do. You come in and sit down, Chance. Would you mind telling me, Mr. Schafft, why your mother just disclaimed all knowledge of Mrs.—of your wife?"

"My mother?" The big man stood still, meeting Eggart's inquiring gaze for some time, and then lowered his body into a nearby chair. "Are you sure that she understood your question? She's rather elderly, you know."

"She understood me quite well. In fact, she repeated the name, and said she did not know any Mrs. Lenore

Bellane."

The bitter smile reappeared again, as briefly.

"Oh, I see. Well, in a way she's correct, Lieutenant. There is no Lenore Bellane, and hasn't been for many years. There is a Lenore Schafft. I'm afraid the point is rather important to my mother."

She came into the room, quiet as ever, as he finished speaking. He said, without getting up, "Mother, I've left Johnny Langley in there alone. Tell Marja to give him a cookie and send him home the back way."

Bott and Mahaney were behind her, the sergeant's incredulous eyes going from one to another of the persons in the room. Mrs. Schafft let her son finish, and then said:

"Son, your wife is dead. Have they told you?"

His hand, lying on one knee, made an unfinished gesture. Then he did get up, awkwardly. "Lenore—dead?"

Bott broke in, "I told Edith, Theo. She's upstairs. Marthe, you'd better go up to her—I'll send the little boy home."

No one moved. Eggart waited until Schafft's head turned towards him, for confirmation.

"How did it happen? When?"

"Last Sunday night. It was in the papers. You didn't see it?"

"No—no. But she was here Sunday—she was here all day! She was perfectly all right!"

"She didn't die a natural death, Mr. Schafft. That's why we're here. She was found Monday morning in her hotel room, with her wrists cut. She had died during the night."

Schafft said, "Oh—God ..." and put his face down in his hands. His mother, as if unwilling to have him observed, moved in front of him and put one hand on his head. When he did not stir, she withdrew it and went without haste toward the front hall.

"Mrs. Schafft!"

"Yes?"

"May I ask where you're going?"

"To my granddaughter."

"Please don't leave the house. I'd like to talk to you later."

"Very well."

When his mother left the room Schafft rose suddenly from his chair, paced over to the concert grand by the windows and dropped heavily on the bench behind it. The piano was closed, and he leaned his heavy arms on the lid and stared down at it.

"I can't believe it—I can't believe Lenore would do such a horrible thing!"

"You say she was here all day Sunday? With you?"

"Yes, yes. From noon until evening."

"She didn't live here?" Schafft shook his head. "You were separated?"

"Not as you mean it, no. She had a position in New York—it was more convenient for her to live there. She used the name Bellane for the same reason—it was better known in New York. I believe the Bellanes are an old family there."

"Where was she employed?"

The heavy brows drew together slightly, and Schafft's voice became remote. "Some cosmetic concern—I don't recall the name of it. Princess Something."

"Princess Natasha," said Bott, from the dining room archway. He added, "I'll go get rid of that kid, Lieutenant."

Eggart nodded, and motioned for Mahaney to remain.

"How long had she been living in New York?"

"I don't know exactly. Since Edith was nine or ten."

"But you say you were not separated?"

"Well, well. Perhaps we were, in one sense. Lenore came here to us when she could, but it wasn't often. She was happy and successful in her work, and it would have been cruel to make her give it up. She was not—domestically inclined."

"Your daughter lives with you?"

"Yes."

"All the time?"

"Yes. She is a student of the piano. It wouldn't do to have her work interrupted."

"What is Mrs.—Schafft's New York address?"

"It was—it was on Twelfth Street. She moved there recently."

Bott came back into the room in time to supply the number, and sat down in the chair Schafft had vacated. He nodded to Barney, who was inconspicuous in one corner, and then frowned at the rug under his feet. Eggart's tone changed slightly.

"Did your wife usually stay at a hotel when she came to visit you?"

"No, never; her room was always waiting for her here. But this summer we have rented it to a young friend of Mr. Bottman's—to Mr. Hm," he added courteously, remembering his roomer's presence. "We were not expecting her to come while he was here. And she could always have shared—one of our rooms. But she said she could remain only one day, and because of that, and the heat, she preferred to stay at a hotel."

"Did you know which one?"

"I—suppose she mentioned it. I don't recall."

"She came up from New York to spend one day here? She had some reason?"

"Not exactly. That is, her reason for coming was not

primarily to visit us. You see, my wife's position entailed a great deal of traveling, on rather strict schedules. Whenever she could, she would arrange to be in Boston on the weekend, so that we might have Sunday together."

"Did she travel alone?"

"Oh, yes."

"She had no companion on this trip?"

"She didn't mention one. I think it was customary for her to make her trips by herself."

"When did you know that she was coming?"

"She called us Sunday morning from the hotel, and told us she would be here for the day."

"Did she come through here on regular schedules?"

"I don't think so."

"Frequently?"

"No—not frequently. Two or three times a year."

"Staying how long?"

An unexpected and slow tide of color came up in Schafft's face.

"A day or so."

There was a short pause. Eggart, who was making notes, turned a page in his notebook.

"Do you recognize this description as one of your wife's friends: a tall, slender man in his forties, heavy dark hair and pale complexion, very well dressed?"

Schafft's bewilderment deepened.

"I—I don't seem to. Why do you ask?"

"That doesn't suggest anyone you know?"

"Not at the moment, no."

"Can you tell me anything of your wife's friends or associates in New York? Any names she may have mentioned?"

"Why—she lived very quietly. Most of the people she came in contact with were business associates. I don't

remember her mentioning one any more than another."

"Do you remember any of their names?"

"No." Raising his head, he asked again, "Why do you
ask about this—this dark-haired man?"

"He was in Mrs. Schafft's company the day she died.
Several of the hotel employees saw them together."

"At the hotel?"

"Yes."

Schafft received this information so impassively that
none of them was prepared for his next action. Without
a word he rose from the piano bench, crossed the room,
and walked through the portieres. A moment later
the door to the music parlor across the hall opened
and closed. Both Eggart and Bott checked Mahaney's
instinctive pursuit—Eggart with a shake of the head,
Bott by getting up in his path.

"Let him go, feller," said Bott gruffly. "That's a pretty
hard thing to have sprung on you all of a sudden."

"No more than he could have read in the papers,"
Eggart reminded him. "If he read the papers."

There was a creaking in the corner as Barney got
up.

"Look, Lieutenant, you don't need me anymore, do
you?"

Eggart said he guessed not, for the moment; but
Bott intercepted his driver on the way out. "Stick
around, son. I'll want you to drive me back."

"You're through driving yourself for today, are you,
Bott?" Eggart remarked. "I'd like to talk to you about
your little excursion this morning—but first, perhaps
you wouldn't mind going upstairs after Mrs. Schafft."

"I don't mind a bit, Lieutenant, but I sure hope you
won't be rough on her—about what she said, I mean.
She's a pretty old lady, and—"

"I've got eyes, Bott. And ears too."

Eggart watched Bott and Barney go out of the room together, and then turned to his sergeant. "Mahaney, call up and tell them I've got hold of Bott, will you? And leave this number in case anything turns up."

Alone in the comfortable, old-fashioned living room, Eggart settled back to wait, looking around with quiet, attentive eyes. The room, like the rest of the house, was probably just as it had been for the last twenty years or more—except for the enormous grand piano at which Schafft had been sitting. That had been acquired within the last five years, Eggart guessed, and not for peanuts. Was it the girl's? She must be pretty good to have outgrown the piano across the hall so young. His speculations went on from one thing to another, with no definite end in view as yet, but only the persistent desire to understand everything with which he came in contact that was Eggart's main characteristic.

Slow footsteps on the stairs interrupted him, and he got to his feet as Mrs. Schafft entered the room. She nodded gravely, and waited for him to speak first.

When he asked her to sit down she hesitated a moment, and then did so. Mahaney came in behind her and settled on a chair near the archway, where he could watch her without meeting that level regard. He jumped as Eggart said abruptly:

"You weren't on very close terms with your daughter-in-law, Mrs. Schafft?"

"I had scarcely seen her for many years."

"You didn't correspond?"

"No. Lenore's interests and mine were far apart."

"Wasn't your granddaughter a common interest?"

"Edith writes her own letters."

"Regularly?"

"I believe so."

"She and her mother were on good terms?"

"Yes."

"Mrs. Schafft was here all day Sunday?"

"All afternoon. She came about noon and left in the early evening."

"Did you speak with her?"

"Certainly," said Mrs. Schafft, with grave rebuke.

"Did you notice anything different in her behavior? Did she mention any change in her present life, or her future plans?"

The old lady considered this so long and carefully that he was not prepared for the brevity of her reply, which was simply, "No."

"She seemed just as usual?"

"I should say so. Lenore was always emotional and highly strung, but no more than usual this time."

"Did she mention any companion?"

This puzzled her. She repeated, "A companion? Here in Boston, you mean?"

"In Boston, yes. Mrs. Schafft had breakfast with a friend of hers that morning, at the hotel. She said nothing of this to any of you?"

For the first time, the old lady's composure seemed shaken. There was complete bewilderment in her blue eyes.

"Breakfast with a friend? But who was this friend?"

"Unfortunately, we haven't discovered that yet. He was a man of about her own age, very dark and with a pale complexion. Do you know anyone who answers that description?"

"No one. Are you sure there isn't some mistake?"

"There's no mistake. They were seen together at the Clyde."

"At the Clyde Hotel? Together?" With a surprisingly

firm movement, she got to her feet and stood there, her hands clasping and unclasping. "You must be mistaken. You must be. Lenore was not a good wife nor a good mother, but she was not a loose woman! If you are trying to suggest that she was, I cannot discuss her with you any longer!"

"Oh, Mrs. Schafft," said Eggart, as she started out of the room. Without turning she answered, "Yes?"

"Will you ask your granddaughter to come down, please?"

From the stiffness of her back he thought she was going to refuse; but without a word of either protest or agreement she started off again, and they heard her climbing the stairs briskly a moment later.

Chapter Six

Mahaney made the face of a boy whose teacher has just left the room. "You don't want to go talking about her family like that, Lieutenant. She don't like it!"

"No, she doesn't, does she? I didn't think she'd take it quite that hard."

"Well, I can see her point. She don't want to make her son out any foolisher than he is. It's bad enough his wife goes off and gets a job in New York, without she brings her fancy man back home with her."

"I think that's about the size of it, Mahaney. People can stand almost anything but being made fools of."

Mahaney looked gratified, and studied his enormous hands with a philosophical air until heavy approaching footsteps made him look up in surprise.

"That little girl must have cleats on, Lieutenant."

"It's Bott again," said Eggart impatiently, and got up as that gentleman's anxious face appeared between the portieres. "Now listen to me, Bott. Your turn will come when it comes, and not before. Right now I want to see that girl—and I mean right now!"

Bott appeared to swallow something, but he managed a tight smile.

"Sure, sure—only you're wasting your time, Eggart. I know what you want to ask her, and I can tell you just as well as she can. Better. What you want is to find out about this Mystery Man, isn't it? Well, I can save you a whole lot of time, because—"

"I'll do my own time-saving," said Eggart ominously. "You tell the young lady to come down—no one's going to hurt her, but I won't promise you the same unless you cut this monkey business out."

"Now listen, Lieutenant—do you want information, or do you just want to upset a lot of innocent people? If you—"

"He wants to talk to me, Bott," a low voice interrupted, and the girl came quietly through the curtains and stood beside him. "And I want to talk to him. Really. Be a dear, and don't make any more fuss. I can't bear it."

He looked at her with nervous exasperation, as if he were going to pick her up and carry her bodily out of the room. She walked away from him and sat down, and he came to lean over the back of her chair, in grim silence.

Eggart said, "Thanks. We don't do this for a hobby, you know."

"Before you ask me things," said the girl, "would you mind telling me how my mother died ? She didn't just—die, did she?"

The unevenness of her voice warned Eggart that her calm was only skin-deep, and largely an illusion produced by the regularity of her features, her level brows, and the neatness of her dark hair. But the expression in her eyes would have gone better with a little dishevelment. He gauged that surface control before he spoke, and decided it would hold.

"No, she didn't just die, Miss Schafft. You haven't seen the morning paper? Or last night's?"

"We only take the evening paper," Bott interrupted, "and nobody reads that regularly but me—and I don't pay much attention to the local items. Now listen to me, Edith honey—you and Theo and I will talk this bad part over later, when you've pulled yourself together a little. Right now all you want to do is get this talk with the lieutenant over and lie down again. Isn't that right, Lieutenant?"

"It might be better that way," Eggart agreed tactfully. "I won't keep you long, but I'm anxious to find out about your mother's visit here Sunday. Did you know she was coming?"

"No, she didn't."

"Bott, for the last time—"

"No, I didn't know," said Edith, and put her strong young hand over Bott's red paw. "None of us knew until she called from the hotel."

"Had you heard from her recently, before that?"

"About a week before. She wrote to me every Sunday. I think this must have been some business matter that came up suddenly, because she always told me where she was going."

"Didn't you ask her why she came so unexpectedly?"

"No," Edith said simply. "I never thought of it—I was just glad to see her."

"Did she seem in good spirits?"

"Yes," she said, and her eyes were suddenly full of tears. "She seemed happy."

"Unusually so?"

The girl hesitated, and Bott said impatiently, "Lenore was kind of moody, Eggart—up and down for no reason. I guess she was kind of pleased at surprising Edith."

"Did your mother talk to you about anyone else? A friend that might be joining her here?"

"A friend?"

"Yes, a nice-looking man about her own age," said Eggart, feeling foolish, "with heavy dark hair and a pale complexion."

"You mean Uncle Francis?" said Edith, staring. "But he wasn't here."

"He was downtown, honey. She was probably going to mention it to you later."

From his new perch on the piano bench, Mahaney burst out: "If he's your uncle, how come your own folks don't recognize him from his description?"

"Now, listen to me, Mahaney! Don't you talk that way—"

"Well, what kind of a family is this, anyway—?"

"Bott! Mahaney! That's enough." Eggart went on gently, to the dazed girl, "We think your uncle was here in Boston, and we'd like to ask him about it. Now, would you mind telling me something about him? What he looks like, for instance?"

"But you know what he looks like—and there isn't anything to tell! I don't know why he was here, and I'm sure mother couldn't have known he was!"

"But what's his name? Where does he live?" Mahaney demanded frantically.

Edith, getting steadily paler, said his name was Francis Bellane, and he lived in New York.

"Your mother's brother?" Eggart asked.

"No, my father's."

Mahaney made strangled sounds from his corner,

and Edith looked at him numbly.

"If you'd let me tell this," Bott interrupted, "and leave Edith alone for a minute—"

"Why don't *you* leave her alone?" asked Mahaney wrathfully. "If you'd come down to headquarters with that driver of yours in the first place, like you'd ought to have done—"

"Oh, please!" Edith cried, and got up. "You won't tell me anything, and you're all quarreling.... What does Uncle Francis have to do with this?"

"That's what we don't know," said Eggart, with a deadly glance at the two red-faced men. "The simplest way to find out would be to ask him; and that's what we'll do, if you'll just tell us where we can get in touch with him. Do you know his address?"

"No, I don't. He lives on Long Island, but I've never been there. But if you're thinking he hurt my mother, or let anyone else hurt her, then you're wrong—you're wrong! He was the best friend she had—she said so over and over again!"

"How does it happen that neither your father nor your grandmother knows him, Miss Schafft?"

"Because they're not related to him," said Edith desperately. "They're not related to me, either—they've just taken care of me for years, and been very good to me. There's no reason why they should know Uncle Francis—the only times I've seen him were when I was in New York visiting mother. He hasn't been here since I was a little girl!"

"Your father's name is Bellane, then? Is he alive?"

"Yes, but I don't know where. And there's no use telling him about mother, because he doesn't care at all."

"When did you last see him?"

"I've never seen him," said Edith bleakly.

"When did you last see your uncle?"

"Last May. I was in New York for a week, and he came to visit us a lot, and took us out."

"How would you describe him?"

For a moment they all thought she was going to break down, and Eggart half closed the notebook on his knee. But from some inner reserve she found a last measure of control, and managed to reply with very little delay and great precision.

"He's a very fine-looking man—tall, and he looks beautiful in his clothes. He has lovely manners, and a lot of black, wavy hair. He says it's so healthy because he never wears hats, even in town. He isn't very healthy, though, even though he looks so strong—the only way you can tell is because he's rather pale, and his eyes always have dark circles under them, but he's always cheerful, and he doesn't complain about his trouble. It's his kidneys," she added, and burst finally into tears.

Eggart put his notebook down, got up, and went to lay a gentle hand on her shoulder.

"All right, Miss Schafft—or is it Miss Bellane? You've been splendid and brave, and I'm very grateful to you. We won't bother you anymore just now, if you'd like to go back to your room."

"Come on, honey. Bott'll take you."

"Sergeant Mahaney will take her," Eggart corrected flatly. "Mr. Bottman will stay right where he is."

Edith settled the matter by slipping between the velvet portieres and running upstairs alone. The atmosphere left behind her was a tense one. Eggart broke it by resuming his seat, picking up the notebook, and saying casually, "All right, Bott. We're ready for you now. What's this explaining you want to do?"

Bott, looking as though what he really wanted to do

was commit mayhem, stood where he was and said gruffly, "What else do you want to know?"

"All about Francis Bellane, and his brother, too. How long ago was the girl's mother divorced?"

"Years. When Edith was a baby."

"What's the father's name?"

"Paul. He's some kind of architect."

"He doesn't contribute to her support?"

"Enough to buy her shoes, maybe. Fifty a month from some lawyer's office. It goes in the bank. Edith doesn't need his money."

"Then Schafft really supports her?"

A peculiar, flat stare settled in Bott's eyes. "We all look after her—Theo, and Marthe, and me. She don't lack for nothing."

"Her mother didn't contribute?"

"Lace underwear," said Bott, in a burst of scorn. "Ten bucks in a letter."

"How about Uncle Francis?"

Bott dismissed Uncle Francis in one rude word. "Edith hardly knew him herself. She visited her mother maybe once or twice a year, and this guy takes them out to dinner, and she thinks he's fine. All right, maybe he is. But she didn't know him much better'n she knows you."

"Her mother knew him pretty well, though?"

"I doubt it. Lenore was pretty proud of her Bellane connections, even though they didn't last very long. She probably roped the guy in to give Edith a good time, and he was too softhearted to refuse."

"Well, let that go. About Sunday. Did you see her while she was here?"

"Sure, at dinner. She was all right. Just like always."

"What did she talk about?"

"Lord, I don't know. Just chatter."

"You didn't like her much, did you?"

"Why should I? She was a scatterbrained, hysterical woman, and no good to anybody. But don't go thinking I'd be crazy enough to kill her. She wasn't that important to me."

"What makes you think anybody killed her?"

Bott laughed shortly. "Keep your secrets, Eggart—I don't want 'em. But if you think Lenore ever carved up her own flesh, you're crazy. She didn't have the nerve."

Eggart made no reply to this, except to tuck his notebook away and stand up.

"What happened to your friend Schafft? He didn't leave the house, did he?"

"No, he's across the hall. What do you want him for?"

"I want him to come down and identify his wife," said Eggart politely. "If that's all right with you."

Unexpectedly Bott grinned.

"Don't be a sorehead, Eggart. You got what you wanted, didn't you?"

"If I didn't, I'll be back. Now go round him up for me, will you?"

Bott shrugged, and went.

Later that afternoon Eggart stopped by his chief's office to report progress.

"A funny thing just happened. This Francis Bellane we've been tracing just called up from New York—wanted the officer in charge of the Bellane case, and got me. Says he's just heard from the New York police, is all cut up, and wants to come here right away and talk about it."

"Well, let him come. You mean he admits being with her?"

"Yes, in the morning. I'm going to wait here in the

building for him tonight, and I thought you might want to sit in."

"If he wants to talk, that means he thinks he's got an alibi," said Captain Cooney shrewdly.

"Could be. This taxi driver says he didn't seem too happy about whatever the woman was saying to him, Sunday. Said she wanted to do it her way, and go ahead. That doesn't sound much like good old Uncle Francis."

"Well, let him talk if he wants to," said Cooney.

"Don't worry," said Eggart. "I will."

Chapter Seven

"Come on in my room and have a beer," said Bott, putting his head around the edge of Barney's door. It was less an invitation than a command, and Barney put down his copy of Moore's *Theory of Aerodynamics*—without too much reluctance—and followed Bott next door.

Eggart and Mahaney had been gone for about half an hour, taking Schafft with them, and the house had gone back to its customary quiet. Barney, hoping that Bott would remember about him when he wanted to be driven somewhere, had stayed in his room and made fitful attempts to read while the questioning went on downstairs. It was a relief not to have to sit in while those very personal interviews took place; but he was inclined to wonder what other family peculiarities had come out.

Bott's hard, closed face gave him no clue. He shut his own door behind Barney, said "Sit down, son," and vanished behind the curtained recess where, Barney knew, were a small electric cooling box and an electric plate. Ordinarily Bott took his meals with the family, but this seemed to be one of the little extra conveniences that accumulate in a room that has been lived in a long while. There were plenty of them. Large as it was, the room seemed stuffed with furniture and possessions; the walls were almost covered with calendar and magazine cut-outs, and everywhere you looked were pictures of Edith. Edith, at every stage of her life; Edith tinted; Edith enormously framed; Edith hanging from the walls and sitting on bureau and desk.

When Bott reappeared, with two opened quarts and two glasses, the first thing Barney asked was, not unnaturally, "Where's Edith?"

Bott gestured with his head. "Over in her room. She's resting, and Marthe's with her, fixing over a black dress for her to wear."

"For the newspaper photos?"

"There won't be any newspaper photos. We're going to take her over to South Boston—my old lady will take good care of her till this blows over. We'd do better to start right now, before Eggart hands out any stories; but when Marthe gets an idea, there's no use arguing with her. And I guess it is better for Edith to wear black."

"Is it all right with Eggart, moving her over there?"

"If it isn't, he can tell me about it," said Bott grimly. He held up his half-empty glass and sighed at it. "I tell you, this whole thing's a problem."

"Did you know her very well, Bott?"

"Who—Lenore? Sure, I guess I knew her longer than anybody. We grew up on the same street, in South Boston. Wouldn't think it, would you—her so refined, and all. But she worked hard at it, Lenore did. Now me, I just don't care. Had too much else to worry about."

"You knew her before she was married to Schafft?"

"To Theo? I knew her before she was married to anybody. Not real well; she was a lot younger. Just the way you know any brat on your own block, where all the kids live in the street most of the time."

"How did you happen to keep in touch with her, then?"

"Well, now, that's a funny thing," said Bott reflectively. "I was thinking about it a little while ago, sitting here waiting for Edith. It sure is funny the way things work out. Especially since Lenore pulled out as early as she could, and went to New York. She was pretty, and had kind of a high singing voice, and I guess she meant to have a career for herself, or something. I don't think the career ever came to much—her old lady and mine were friends, but I didn't pay much attention to what they'd be telling me. All I remember is that she'd keep asking for money, and a couple of times her old lady borrowed it off me to send her. Then all of a sudden she married this Bellane fellow."

"I didn't know she'd been married before."

"Sure. Edith's name is Bellane—didn't you know that?"

"I thought Schafft was her father."

"Lord, no. Lenore picked herself a real fancy husband first time—a New York fellow, real social. Her old lady was tickled pink—for a while there she was over to the house every night, pretty near, talking about it."

"What happened to him?"

"Oh, she left him. Or he put her out, more likely. Anyway she was back at her mother's before Edith was six months old, and Edith with her. I never have been able to figure what kind of a fellow Bellane must have been, to let his only kid get away like that. And never even came after her!"

"He didn't?"

"Not once. The brother was around some, trying to patch things up, I guess, but Lenore stayed on, and he went back, and by and by her old lady let out that she was having a divorce. I never did know just what the arrangement was, except that it was a funny one. Lenore had Edith, but not much money. You could tell that, because she went on living there with her mother, and she wouldn't have done that unless she'd had to. I remember how restless she was, and how she used to come over a lot in the evenings, with Edith. We liked the baby, mom and me, and Lenore could tell it.

"Well, things went on that way till Lenore's mother died. Lenore was taking singing lessons, and filling in any singing jobs she could find, and the way it turned out was that my old lady was taking care of the baby more'n half the time, with Lenore's mother sick. When she died, we had to take Lenore in too. There was just the two of us, so we had room. We weren't real happy about the setup, but somebody had to take care of that baby, and we were darned sure Lenore wouldn't. And the baby was company for mom during the day, and for me in the evening."

Bott stopped, poured the last of the quart bottle into his glass, and grinned a little wryly. "That's the way it was, for better than five years. I wouldn't be surprised if that's how I wound up an old batch. There ain't many girls willing to take on a fellow with a baby—specially if the baby's got a mother right there. And I sure wouldn't have traded Edith for any girl I knew!"

"You could have married one of Edith's rivals, and got yourself a reasonable facsimile."

Bott grinned again, more cheerfully, and absently

picked up Barney's half-full bottle. "Sure, and what if I'd got me a boy? Or an old redhead like me? I'll tell you, you just don't realize the kind of a baby Edith was! Why, she was talking plain as you before she was two! And sing? Say—" He checked himself, and said flatly, "Well, anyhow, I done it this way, and I'm not sorry."

"I shouldn't think you would be. It seems to have worked out pretty nicely. About Edith," Barney added, remembering Lenore's remarkably unlamented death.

"Well, yes," said Bott; and then, "Course, things don't just work themselves out like you want—you have to help them a little. There was one pretty mean thing I did, back there, but I can't say I'm sorry. When Lenore married Theo, that was."

"Nothing illegal, I hope."

"No, no. Real legal. Lenore owed me a pretty big sum of money by then. She'd been taking voice training, and it was mighty expensive. The money Bellane sent for the baby wouldn't stretch, so she began borrowing from me again. I didn't much want to pass out my money that way—it didn't come too easy, and I had plenty of use for it—but on the other hand, I didn't want her to pick up Edith and leave. So I lent it to her, and she had her lessons. Years of 'em. And then when Edith was six, and just starting school, Lenore decided she was going to leave and marry Theo.

"I didn't know him, or anything about him, except he was one of her musician friends. She told me he had a nice big house, and could give Edith a home, and good-bye, Mr. Bottman—thank you very much. Just about like that. I got pretty sore," said Bott reflectively.

Watching the powerful hand gripping Bott's glass, and the heavy red face that bent to drink from it, Barney didn't doubt it. He couldn't imagine that flutelike voice talking down Bott when he was "pretty sore."

"You never considered marrying her yourself, Bott?"

"I did not," Bott said with emphasis. There was a silence; evidently that was the end of that topic. Barney refilled his glass, and waited.

"I had these notes of hers," Bott went on presently. "Real businesslike; that was Lenore for you, when both of us knew I'd never ask for the money or get it, without a miracle. Well, anyway, I had 'em. And I told Lenore they had to be paid up before she left. I knew Theo wasn't any millionaire, and even if he was it would take pretty much nerve to hit a fellow for a couple of thousand before you were even married."

"A couple of thousand?"

"Damn' close to three." Bott laughed suddenly, with perfect good humor. "I never have seen that money, Barney, and I guess I never will. Never expected to. I just hoped it might keep her from romping out in too much of a hurry."

"And did it?"

"Well, things worked out, in time." Bott looked slowly around his room, nodding, more to himself than to Barney. "She didn't object to my visiting over here, after they were married, and I used to take Edith out on holidays. Sometimes the folks came along too. We hit it off right away, luckily—I like refined folks, when they don't have it hanging all over 'em, if you know what I mean. And Theo's kind of a solitary fellow—he likes company, but he won't go after it. That kind."

Whether it was the beer, or Bott's long, solemn recounting of this fantastic relationship, Barney found himself wanting to grin at nothing in particular. He took a long swallow, and said, "Well, I'm glad it did work out. How did you happen to—to move in?"

"Oh, it just came around that way. I could see they had a nice big house here, and I kind of sounded Lenore out. She mentioned it to the folks, and they were agreeable. It's been a mighty fine arrangement— I've never regretted it, and I don't think they have either. Specially after Lenore left. It made company for Theo—somebody to talk to."

"And company for Edith."

"Oh, I'm no company for her," said Bott modestly. "Edith's 'way ahead of me, now. But she knows her old Bott is right here, looking out for her every minute. She's going a long ways, and I'm going to see she has everything she needs to get there. That's about all an old roughneck like me is good for."

He made this humble disclaimer with unconcealed satisfaction, and Barney's amusement died. There was no doubt it was true, that everything he had or could do was at the girl's disposal; but there was also no doubt that Bott meant to go right along behind his charge, every step of her "long ways." In a parent this would have been understandable, and a little sad. In Bott, the "old batch," it was almost frightening. Barney was reminded for a moment of the legendary wild beast who makes off with a human child and rears it with passionate devotion in its own den. But woe to the other humans who intrude—and woe too, no doubt, to the little human itself should it try to escape.

The next minute he was ashamed of this idle whimsy. The "little human" had certainly had nothing but kindness so far, and Barney himself was gathering in his share of that same kindness. Not without a fair return on his own part, of course. He was a good driver, and he paid his way here, in Bott's home. Nevertheless Bott's goodwill, if a little heavy-handed at times, had been of definite help.

Just as Barney was beginning to feel annoyed with himself, Bott added: "I bought her that big piano downstairs, a couple of years ago. Three thousand dollars—best on the market." He picked up Barney's bottle again, discovered it was empty too, and got up. "Well, let's see what's going on in Edith's room. Come on; she must be about ready."

Without waiting for Barney's reply, he went out into the hall and rapped sharply on Edith's door. As Barney came up behind him the door opened a few inches and Marja, the Polish maid, peered out. Her dark young face was twisted with the incoherent excitement that sometimes erupted into fits, as Barney had learned one night soon after his arrival; but the discipline of the house had reached her too, and most of her chaotic energy was spent on mops and brushes.

Her eyes went past Bott to Barney, who was an especial object of wonderment to her, and widened joyfully. She pulled the door back at once, to disclose Edith standing in the middle of the room in her slip, while Mrs. Schafft lowered a black dress over her head. The old lady turned her head sharply, and exclaimed:

"Marja! No!"

The maid's face clouded with instant distress, the door shut hastily, and Bott turned to Barney with a chuckle.

"She's kind of a loony, I guess you've noticed. But she's a good worker, and Marthe got her cheap from some home."

"That's fine," said Barney. "Maybe we'd better go back and wait."

"No, no. They're nearly ready."

When they were admitted, a few minutes later, Edith

was still standing in the middle of the room while Marthe put the last touches to her frock. It was simple and beautifully fitting, with short sleeves and a round neck; so well made that its unrelieved black was not at all oppressive. Bott circled the girl, making admiring sounds.

"You did fine, Marthe. Fine!"

"She always does," said Edith, smiling at the older woman. It was a tired little smile, and the girl's eyes did not have much part in it, but affection was there. "Are you driving us over, Barney?"

She used his name for the first time, and with deliberation, as if aware of his reluctance to be present. He said he was, whenever they were ready.

"I'm ready now, but I'd much rather not go. Granny, you know I'd be much easier here with all of you. I'll stay in my room—those reporters won't even know I'm here! Please?"

Mrs. Schafft shook her head once. "No, Edith." That was all. The girl's smile died, and she picked up her black handbag from the bed. Bott took it away from her.

"I'll take your things down, honey. Come on—let's get going." At his touch on her bare arm, Edith moved forward obediently. Mrs. Schafft hesitated, glancing around the large, pleasant room before following them. Marja, her black eyes going from one to another, was busy cleaning away the sewing effects, and Mrs. Schafft left her there, closing the door firmly.

Edith and Bott were already on the stairs, and Barney waited for Mrs. Schafft to follow them; but she remained standing at his side in the hall, her calm eyes on his face. After a moment she said, "It was you who drove her here, wasn't it?"

"Mrs.—Mrs. Schafft? Yes, it was." When she did not

speak, he added, "I'm sorry. I know all this has been hard for you."

She moved forward as if she had not heard, and started down the stairs. At the landing she let him come up with her, and remarked, in the same tone, "Your rent was due yesterday."

Barney adjusted to this, reached for his wallet, and then paused, scenting eviction. "I know—it slipped my mind. Shall I pay you now, or would you rather I found another room?"

"Another room?"

Something happened then that he was completely unprepared for. The first smile he had seen her give touched her mouth briefly and then smoothed away. She said, "Whatever you like," and went on down-stairs.

On his way out the door he gravely handed her a five and a one, and in return she took a slip of paper from her pocket and gave it to him. Going down the walk he discovered it to be one of the usual rent re-ceipts, filled out and dated the previous day.

Chapter Eight

Partly for policy's sake, and partly because Cooney hadn't turned up, Eggart kept Francis Bellane waiting nearly half an hour that evening. He had originally meant to keep him even longer, in the antiseptic-look-ing waiting room, but his own curiosity got the better of him.

The first thing he noticed about Bellane was that he was still hatless. Otherwise his dress and appearance were impeccable, and the uncovered dark head gave him an air of being in his own office. He was as much at ease as if he had been; and Eggart found himself, with wry amusement, standing up to shake hands in response to the other's offer. The man was certainly handsome, with his regular features and dark, expressive eyes. His forty-odd years had left less trace on him than the refractory kidneys Edith had mentioned so tearfully, and he showed no resentment or impatience at the long wait.

"It's good of you to see me. I know a thing like this must keep you busy."

"I'm not seeing you just out of good nature, Mr. Bellane," said Eggart. "In fact, if you hadn't come down I'd have asked you to." He was annoyed to find his manner echoing Bellane's, and added: "We've gone to a lot of trouble tracing you."

"I know, and I'm sorry for it. But I had no idea ... Tell me, how did it happen?"

"Don't you read the papers either, Mr. Bellane?"

"The papers?" he repeated, taken aback, and then touched his full lower lip with a pale tongue. "Yes, of course. It would be in the papers, wouldn't it. Poor Lenore. No, I've been too upset to read since I heard the news. Is it possible that she really—really cut her wrists open?"

"Doesn't it seem possible to you?"

Bellane shook his head.

"No. She was a woman of strong impulses, and her nerves were not all they might have been, but a brutal thing like this—no, I can't imagine it in connection with Lenore."

"You knew her well?"

"I had known her over a long period of years," said Bellane, with the air of one making a distinction. "She was my brother's wife, you know; and while we lost touch after she and Paul split up, I ran into her again when she came back to New York. She didn't have an easy time, poor girl, and I was glad to do what I could for her."

"And what was that?" Eggart inquired.

"Why—nothing too impressive, I suppose. She was alone there in town, and there were times when she needed a little advice or assistance, or perhaps just companionship. And when her daughter was there, she liked a little help in entertaining her."

"I see," said Eggart. "Now what about last Sunday?"

"Of course. It sounds a little confused, I'd better warn you, but it's really simple enough. You see, Lenore was extremely fond of her daughter, but she realized that to take Edith out of the—the home she is now in would have been unwise, in view of her own circumstances. At the same time, she herself didn't feel that she should come back here to live. She was successful in her work, and I don't think she was very happy with these people. They're good, and kind, I suppose, but a little oppressive to live with—"

"For the girl's mother, you mean," Eggart interrupted.

Bellane started, and then caught the other's meaning. His dark brows came together momentarily, and Eggart thought "Temper," with satisfaction.

"Edith seems quite fond of them," he said coldly. "After all, she's a child, and lives mainly in a world of her own. Lenore would certainly not have left her there if the child had been unhappy."

"About Sunday," said Eggart. "And we might as well get this on record." He flipped the key of his intercommunication box, spoke into it, and settled back to wait for the stenographer. Bellane, watching all this with mild interest, offered Eggart a cigarette and lit one for himself.

When the police stenographer had come in, chosen

a place, and settled himself to write, Bellane turned to him and said courteously, "I'll make this as clear as I can, but you may stop me if you find it necessary."

The man started, and then grinned.

"You just talk, mister, and don't worry about me."

Deliberately, Eggart took him back over old ground. "Just put your previous relationship with Mrs. Schafft into form—with dates, if possible."

Bellane drew a small leather notebook from his inside coat pocket. "As a matter of fact, that's just what I did on the train. I understand the official records must be exact, and I'll try to keep them that way. Very well, then; as nearly as I can remember, here it is." There was a slight delay while he took a pair of glasses from their case and put them on; they sobered his romantic appearance considerably, as did the concise, thoughtful air with which he translated his notes.

It appeared that he had first met his brother's wife at the time of their marriage, and had seen her quite frequently during that time—a little less than two years—and then had lost touch with her for about six or seven years. After that they had met by accident in New York, and Lenore had told him she was married again, but filling a singing engagement there in town. He was surprised, as he had thought his brother had provided for her comfortably, to find out that she needed the money she was earning. Feeling a family responsibility, he had told her to call on him for help if she should need it.

"In spite of the fact she was married again?"

"I gathered that her new husband wasn't much help."

"Did you. And then?"

"Then," Bellane resumed his perusal of the notes, "then she did get in touch with me, several months later. The singing engagement was over, and no other was in prospect. She didn't want to go back to Boston, and asked me to help her find another. Unfortunately, I haven't any influence at all in theatrical matters," said Bellane, smiling, "and I told her so, and offered her a loan. She accepted it, and I heard no more from her for a time. Then she wrote me from Boston and said she would be willing to take any kind of position that would give her an independent income, and asked if I knew of any.

"It happened that my wife had an interest in a large cosmetic concern, and I was able to arrange for Lenore to have a course of training in the business and a fairly responsible position afterwards. She seemed very pleased, and I know that she has done her work well. She kept the position up to the time of her death.

"Now we come to last Sunday," said Bellane, and turned a page. "You remember I told you she was upset about Edith—about being forced to live apart from her. Well, to a woman of emotional and nervous temperament, that situation can become very wearing. Lenore would frequently have periods of great depression, trying to decide what to do, and she had got in the habit of coming to me for advice. I told her that if she wanted to bring Edith to New York, I would arrange for her to continue her lessons and would see that she had a suitable piano. She's a very talented little girl, you know."

"I gathered that."

"Did you? I suppose they're rather proud of her out there, eh? Well, Lenore was afraid to take the risk. She thought if she took her from her present home and then found she couldn't keep her, they would both end up in disaster."

"Just a minute, Mr. Bellane. Where is Edith's father, in all this? Wouldn't he have been willing to help?"

Bellane's dark eyes, magnified by the glasses, stared at him solemnly. "I'm afraid not. It's painful to tell you this, Lieutenant, but my brother treated Lenore rather badly at the time of their divorce. He took advantage—there's no other word for it—of her desire to be free, and drove a very sharp bargain with her."

"Why was she so anxious to be free?"

"Well, she was angry, I suppose, and impulsive too. They didn't part very amicably."

"Even so, she could have asked for another settlement later, in view of the child."

"Lenore would never have done that," said Bellane decisively. "Never. She was far too proud. In a way, that was why I felt somewhat responsible for her."

"Well," said Eggart, "let's get back to Sunday."

"Yes. Or to Saturday, really. Lenore wired me then, from here. I haven't been able to find the telegram, but I'm sure the telegraph company would have a record. The general effect of the message was that Lenore was in some sort of trouble over Edith, and wanted me to join her here at once."

"You didn't know she was here before that?"

"No. I hadn't seen her in some time." He sighed. "Frankly, I wasn't very anxious to come. I couldn't see why Edith would be in any trouble—these people take good care of her. But on the other hand, if something had gone wrong, and I didn't go—you see. The best thing seemed to be to go, and get it over with. I caught the late train, and got in here about seven-thirty in the morning, and went over to the Standish, where I always stay here in town."

"You knew where Mrs. Bellane was staying?"

"Oh, yes. I called her there, after I'd had breakfast and cleaned up, and she asked me to come over and meet her there, in the dining room. I did, and found her still upset. But for some reason she wouldn't give me any clear account of what was wrong. She was going out to the house, and wanted me to come with her, but she wouldn't explain why. I got irritated with her, God forgive me. She admitted Edith was in good health, and so on, and it began to look to me like another one of Lenore's emotional sprees—except that she wanted me in on it.

"Well, I went up to her room with her after breakfast, thinking she might tell me something more definite in private, but she didn't. I said I wouldn't go out to the house with her unless I knew exactly what I was getting into, and she said I didn't trust her, and began to cry, and the whole thing was a mess. Finally she said she would go alone if I would wait for her. I wouldn't promise, and after she left for Brookline, it seemed clear to me that waiting around there all day was simply insane. So I pulled out, and went home."

"You left Boston? When?"

"Later in the afternoon. I caught the two o'clock train, and got home at seven."

"What did you do then?" said Eggart carefully. Bellane shrugged.

"Went out to my house. I was worn out with so much train-riding, and not in a very good mood. Besides, I half expected some more messages, but there weren't any. I waited around at home all evening, and finally turned in. If she'd only given me some definite explanation, or if she'd been a more balanced person, I'd never in the world—"

"Yes. Did you see anyone at home, Sunday evening?"

"See anyone? No, I was alone."

"Was your wife there? Any servants?"

"I'm a widower," said Bellane, looking as if he began to understand. "I see what you mean, but the only person I talked to was my butler, Graves. He let me in, and later on brought me something to eat. But surely some of the train officials will remember my having been on it."

"At what time did you last see your butler?"

"Oh—eight or so, when I went upstairs. Graves would probably remember."

"You saw no one after that?"

Bellane seemed at a loss, but still polite. "No, I just read a while, and turned in. A friend of mine called me up soon after I got home," he added. "I can let you have his name, if necessary."

Eggart said he would like to have it, and wrote down the august name of a well-known vice-president of Magnum Steel.

"What time would you say he called?"

"Around nine, but I can't swear to it. Graves may have made a note, or remember."

He looked slightly offended at this prying, and volunteered no more information. Eggart asked for his business and home addresses, his age, and his occupation—stockbroker—and then went back over Bellane's interview with his brother's ex-wife, trying for some definite scraps of information. Nothing emerged, except Bellane's conviction that Lenore had been in a very bad state, and should have trusted him more, and so on. He had long ago shut up his little leather notebook, and removed his glasses. Finally Eggart gave up, and let him go.

"I'm planning to stop over in Boston a day or so, if that's all right with you people. I'd like to see Edith, of course, and attend the funeral, and so on."

Eggart said gravely that that was perfectly all right, and asked where he meant to stay. Bellane said at the Standish, and waited without haste to be dismissed.

When the door closed behind him, a little after nine, Eggart at once arranged for day and night surveillance of Mr. Francis Bellane. After that he called Dr. Marshall, of the M. E.'s office, who was handling Lenore Bellane's autopsy.

"I know you can't give me any split-second timing," he began, "but I'd like to know how closely you can figure the time those wounds were made. As late as three A.M.?"

Marshall said it was possible, but that he thought it had been earlier. "No later, certainly," he added; and Eggart thanked him and hung up.

Like most men, he was sensitive to his own mannerisms in other people; and while the grave courtesy that was his own stock-in-trade was a long way from Bellane's punctilio, he was aware that such traits tend to exaggerate themselves under stress. It was his opinion that Bellane's performance that night had been exaggerated to the point of burlesque; he was willing to bet that the vice-president of Magnum Steel would have been amazed to sit in on it. That and several other facets of Bellane's interview interested him just then more than the statement Bellane had made; but it was the statement that called for immediate checking and he got this process under way.

On his way out, half an hour later, he ran into Cooney in the outer office.

"I missed him, huh? Got tied up. How does he figure?"

"He figures himself out, but I'm not sure. He alibis himself in New York up to around nine, but he could have just made it back here in time. Says his trip was a run-around—she wired him Saturday night to come, and then wouldn't tell him right away what was the matter, so he got sore and went home. Took the two o'-clock train, that afternoon, and wants us to check on it."

"Well, we will," said Cooney. "You can go after your own ideas at the same time. What's he like?"

"Pretty," said Eggart, with a bitterness that surprised himself. "Silk underwear, and a regular masseur, and a tailor whose scissors won't work under a hundred and fifty."

Cooney grinned. "Playboy, huh? Well, send his statement up to me first thing in the morning. Where are you off to?"

"The family in Brookline. Just routine stuff. I'll tell you about it tomorrow—want to catch them before they turn in."

"And where's Bellane?"

Eggart told him, and of his own precautions to see that Bellane stayed there. Cooney looked vaguely dissatisfied, as was his wont when nobody had been arrested, and Eggart left him breaking pencil points thoughtfully on Mahaney's desk top.

Chapter Nine

The house on Waterford Street was in a mild state of siege when he got there. The story of Lenore Bellane-Schafft's Brookline family had been given out in time to make the late afternoon editions, and the street was filled with the curious, on foot and in automobiles. Two reporters accosted Eggart on the front porch.

He said, "Where have you been? The Mystery Man's in town—all the other boys just got the story!" But they waited, disconsolate and suspicious, until the dark house received him and shut them out.

There were no lights showing in the front rooms or in the hall itself; it was only after a long delay and persistent bell-ringing that Bott appeared, and led him through the dark living room to the closed-off dining room behind it.

Schafft and his mother were there, seated at the round table on which there was no food or drink. Bott's chair was pushed back; he drew out another for Eggart, and reseated himself.

"We're just sitting here," he explained, "trying to talk some sense into this thing."

Mrs. Schafft's clear eyes acknowledged the lieutenant's presence calmly; he did not think she had been doing much of the talking, or was likely to. Her son raised his untidy head and gave a short laugh.

"Sense! You can't invent sense where there is none. Might just as well sit down and try to improvise a theme, when you don't know what key it's supposed to be in, or what instrument it's for, or what mood it's meant to express.... There's no pattern to life any more ... no requirement, except to make your own particular little noise, and keep on making it. People live their lives now the way a child picks out a tune—hit one key, and then another—any old key. If it makes a bad noise, try again. Nobody's listening anyhow...."

Bott said yes, it was a hard old world, all right, and then turned to Eggart. "Well, what's on your mind, Lieutenant?"

Eggart said he had dropped by to pick up the handwriting specimen Schafft had promised him earlier in the day, and the big man got up without a word and went out of the room. Mrs. Schafft asked if he had brought Lenore's last letter with him, and he said he had not.

"I should like to have seen it, too," she said quietly. "Will it be returned to us?"

Eggart said he thought so, and there was silence—restless on Bott's part, remote on the old lady's—until Schafft returned and handed over a folded double sheet of pale blue notepaper, covered with handwriting. A glance showed that the writing was familiar, and that the letter was dated "Christmas Eve" and began: "My dear Family, How disappointed I am to think we cannot be together …" He folded it, and slipped it into his pocket with a word of thanks.

"I've just been talking to Francis Bellane," he added. "He tells me that Mrs. Schafft sent him a wire last Saturday night, asking him to join her here in Boston. The message said it was 'imperative for Edith's welfare' that he show up."

The deepset eyes of both Schafft and his mother, alike except that the son's seemed curiously older, turned on Eggart with startled attention. Bott exclaimed, "Edith's *welfare!*"

"Yes. What did she mean by that?"

"How would I know? The only trouble Edith ever had was her own mother, to tell you God's truth," said Bott wrathfully. "Why, she hadn't even seen Edith Saturday night!"

"Had she been in communication with any of you?"

"We didn't know she was here, until she called Sunday morning. No, nor we hadn't heard a word from her!" The Schaffts confirmed this with silent nods; Eggart said it was hard to believe she would have sent such a telegram without reason.

"We've already told you there was no reason," said Schafft wearily. "No matter how many different ways you ask, or we answer, the fact doesn't change. Edith was perfectly all right. I suppose that this Bellane was the man with Lenore?"

"Yes. You know him?"

"I met him once, years ago, when he came here with Lenore to see Edith. I hardly remember what he looked like, except that I didn't care for him at the time. I can't conceive that Lenore should have asked him to meet her here, without telling us."

"Yet apparently she did."

Bott growled, "Don't let that fellow fill you up with a lot of stories, Eggart."

"We check on all our information, naturally. The telegram certainly was sent."

"It's completely mad," said Schafft, in a dull voice.

"When she came out here next day, she was still under a big strain. Surely you people must have noticed something!"

"If Lenore did not mean for us to notice, we would not," said Mrs. Schafft unexpectedly. "She knew how to keep her secrets."

"Why do you say that? Had she been keeping secrets that you were aware of?"

"I know of one."

"Mother, what good does it do ...?"

"Please, son. When Lenore first went to New York, Lieutenant, it was because she had been offered a singing engagement. My son is a musician, and he could understand how important that would seem to her. He made no objections at all. But she had been gone nearly a year before we learned that the singing engagement was only a temporary one, and that she had been staying on afterwards for some reason of her own. That wasn't an easy deception to keep up, you can understand, with letters going back and forth every week. But she managed it."

Eggart turned to Schafft, who was listening with

his shaggy brows drawn together in silent displeasure. "This peculiar behavior of your wife's never led to talk of a divorce, Mr. Schafft?"

"You're investigating my wife's death, not her life," he said shortly. "Her behavior may seem peculiar to you; I suppose mine does too. She was not a conventional woman, and I'm not a conventional man."

"Then no divorce was considered?"

"No."

"Not on her last visit here?"

"Mr. Bellane to the contrary, I suppose—no."

"Did she mention taking her daughter back to New York with her?"

"Certainly not," Bott interrupted. "Edith was just there in May. She can't drop her studies every couple of months, even for Lenore's whims. That little girl is a serious worker."

"I don't mean for a visit. I mean permanently."

Bott pushed back his chair impatiently. "That's the craziest yet. The last thing in the world Lenore wanted was to have Edith on her hands permanently!"

"Was it?"

"Well, how would she have supported her? Her job just about kept Lenore comfortable herself—and she never was any good at handling money. And who'd look after Edith when she was away on all those trips? Why, it's insane! Besides, with Edith here, this was one place Lenore could always count on coming back to, and don't think she didn't know it!"

This frank statement did not seem to please either of the Schaffts. The music teacher said coldly, "You still seem to believe that my wife and I were in some disagreement over Edith's custody, or that we were keeping her here against her mother's will. Neither one of these things is true. I don't see what Bellane's purpose is in suggesting them."

"Well, I do," Bott declared. "He's in the hot seat, and he knows it. I suppose he's turned up with a nice fancy alibi?"

"He's accounted for his movements; yes. Which reminds me that I haven't asked you people about Sunday night, after Mrs. B—Schafft left.

"You didn't miss much," said Bott, with an attempt at humor. "We had supper, and went to bed. That's about all."

"The three of you spent the evening together?"

"The four of us. Edith was doing some kind of paper work on her music, and Theo was helping her."

"Hardly that," said Schafft. "Some of the things Edith brings home now are as new to me as to her."

"Anyhow, I listened a while, and had a little snooze in my chair. Marthe was out in the kitchen with Marja, till about nine. Then she came in and sent us all to bed."

"At nine?"

"Well, we're kind of hard to get started. I guess we didn't go up till around ten. That's our usual hour."

"In that case, I won't keep you any longer," said Eggart, rising. "I'll take this letter along, Mr. Schafft, and you'll get it back as soon as our people have finished with it."

"And the other—the other letter?"

"You still think it was written for you?"

"Who else?"

"Someone who understood what she was writing about," said Eggart evenly. "Someone who had recently had a very serious conversation with her—perhaps one that wasn't finished, so that they still needed 'another chance to talk.' You say that person isn't you, Mr. Schafft."

Schafft's color gradually faded while the other spoke; but his deep eyes remained steady and hostile.

"For me, my wife's letter is perfectly clear and plain. You don't understand her, so I'm not surprised that you don't understand her letter. But I do, and I'd like it back."

For a moment Eggart's temptation was strong to break that stubborn reserve, to let Schafft know that the police no longer regarded the letter as a suicide note, and that therefore the "decision" mentioned no longer explained itself. But the Medical Examiner's report was not yet public, and until it was, he, Eggart, was a man ostensibly looking for the dead woman's motives and no one else's.

Bott's shrewd, secretive eyes measured his brief hesitation. "I'm keeping quiet, but it's a little harder for you, isn't it?" they seemed to say. Eggart met them and turned away, his temptation suddenly gone, and Bott got up once more.

"I'll see you out, Eggart—you're liable to bump your shins in that living room." In the front hall, with his hand on the doorknob, he said awkwardly, "I'm glad you're handling this—a nice, refined fellow like you, I mean, that knows how to treat nice people. Cooney, now—I got nothing to say against Cooney, only he ain't never been really happy since he lost his nightstick. I'd sure a lot rather see you out here than him."

"Maybe there's not so much difference as you think, Bott," said Eggart drily. "Don't forget I take my orders from Cooney—and you'd be surprised what he can do without a nightstick."

"Sure, sure. Like I say, he's a good guy—I got nothing against him. All I say is, if we got to have police around the house, I'm glad you're it."

"Well, don't buy me any flowers till we see how this

thing breaks," Eggart warned him, and went out the door with Bott's good-humored chuckle in his ears.

Chapter Ten

Even from an upstairs room, at the back of the house, Waterford Street's sudden popularity was audible. The echo of footsteps drifted back into the dark air over the garden, as did the sound of idling car motors and indistinct human speech.

Barney, his chair and lamp close by the window to catch what breezes might be stirring, had been aware of this undertone of activity all evening long. With his heavy textbook propped on one bare leg, and his bare toes waggling against the cool wood floor, he found himself more inclined to listen and speculate than to pay attention to his own affairs.

The late papers, which he had read over his dinner and been careful not to bring home with him, had carried the story of Lenore Bellane's Brookline family in some detail. There had been pictures of Schafft, head down and somber; of the house; even one of Barney, snapped as he had left headquarters late that afternoon after making a formal statement. Mrs. Schafft, Bott and Edith had escaped the photographers; and it now seemed that Edith was also escaping this grisly paying-of-respects that was going on in the street beneath her windows.

For her sake, he was glad. It gave you a rather sour feeling toward your brothers, to find them treating you like an animal in the zoo. And yet he wondered how long Edith's protection would be able to last—how long they could go on keeping everything from her, even the newspaper stories. From what he had seen and heard of Edith, he didn't think it would be long. Perhaps she already knew more than she was meant to, and was keeping up a protection of her own against the family's distress at knowing how much she knew.

Barney, whose own family relationships had been sufficiently entangled before they petered out altogether, felt almost conventional compared to Edith. For himself, he had only a remarried mother, and a father who had willed his custody to a maiden aunt, on her last legs then, and subsequently deceased. But here was Edith with a father she had never seen and a mother who turned her over, apparently, to any well-disposed person who happened to be around. The odd thing was that there should have been so many well-disposed persons. Edith's makeshift family could not have been more doting if she had been born to them.

Schafft's care of his wife's child Barney could vaguely understand; it might have begun as a general fondness for children (he had infinite patience with his little pupils) and a sense of duty, and then been strengthened by Edith's growing talent, and his pride in that talent. As for the old lady, Barney thought she would have backed her son in whatever he undertook. And she, too, might have grown fond of the little girl.

But Bott was the puzzle. He was not just fond of Edith; she seemed to be an obsession with him. It was as though his fight to keep her near him all these years had ended by being his whole reason for existence. To Bott, Edith seemed to be more valuable than even his own child could have been; she was some kind of a symbol for that lonely, hard-bitten ex-taxi-driver, but what the symbol was Barney did not know. He was not even sure that Bott himself knew.

But whatever the reason for Bott's struggle, he had

been successful so far. And the removal of Lenore meant one rival less to struggle against.

The idea gave Barney a small, queer shock. He closed his book, giving up the attempt to pay attention to it, and reached up to switch off the steady, hot glare of electricity over his head. As he did so, someone tapped lightly at his door.

He said "Yes?" and waited. No answer; but the light tap was repeated. It wasn't Bott. If Edith hadn't been gone, he would have said it was she; in any case, it was someone who required his wearing pants and a shirt. He switched on the light again, reached for his discarded clothes, and said "Just a minute." Presently, still buttoning his hastily tucked-in shirt, he crossed the room and opened the door.

The dark, intent face of Mrs. Schafft's maid peered in at him. She smiled eagerly, and her hands made an involuntary upward movement—those tenacious, affectionate hands from which he was obliged to free his trouser-cuffs and sleeves whenever he passed Marja alone at her work. He discovered his bare feet, too, a moment after Marja did, and moved them back a little. He said, trying not to sound as impatient as he felt, "Well, Marja, what is it?"

The bright, secret gaze left his feet to travel quickly around the room behind him, and settled on his face.

"The policeman is here some more, Meester Barney. A long time."

"Well, that's all right. He won't hurt you."

"He might," said Marja hopefully. "He is very beeg, and I think he will have a gun."

"If he has, he won't use it here. Aren't you supposed to be upstairs in bed?"

One of the hovering hands caught his sleeve before he could get it away. Marja laughed, and then grew sober at once. Her glance flicked away, out toward the hall, and then returned.

"I think that policeman is angry. I think he will come back."

"Angry at you?"

"Oh, no!" She let him have his sleeve back, with unexpected docility, but advanced a couple of steps in giving it up. "I come in?"

"No, Marja. Go on up to bed. The policeman won't hurt you."

He should, he saw, have left it at "No." Any qualification Marja took as encouragement, and she was an expert sidler. The only way to stop that oblique advance was to get in front of it, which made him a fine objective for Marja's quick hands. He counterattacked with a good grip on her shoulders and wheeled her around, at which Marja gasped joyfully.

"Now get," he said, marching her toward the attic stairs. "Do you want Mrs. Schafft to come up and throw us both out? Do you?"

Marja bubbled with suppressed laughter, and grew helpless under it. He got her as far as the first step before the laughter died, and her sturdy body stiffened in resistance.

"No, no!"

"Oh, yes. Right upstairs."

"Marja afraid," she said, suddenly turning a very pitiful face to him. He groped for the attic stair light and found it; the result was a gloomy trickle of illumination from somewhere above.

"There's nothing to be afraid of, Marja. Go on."

She went on peering into his face, which he kept as stern as possible, and her woe deepened. There was no more pushing going on now; she was limp against him, like an unwanted puppy.

"The devil will come here, Meester Barney. Maybe here now. I stay with you."

"The devil won't come here, Marja. He's too busy."

"He come here, all right. Meester Theo tell bad lie, I hear him. The devil will come here to punish. Maybe here now!"

"The devil doesn't punish liars; he likes them," said Barney desperately—and then hesitated. "What kind of lie?"

He asked against his better judgment, which was immediately confirmed. A kind of sly delight replaced Marja's objection, as if Barney had just fallen into a cunning trap.

"Bad lie," she said cheerfully. "I stay with you?"

"You do not. A fine kind of blackmail! I'm surprised at you, Marja."

Marja looked enchanted. After a momentary struggle, he laughed—and then stepped back hastily. But Marja's hands were still; the attention she had gained evidently satisfied her for the moment. He said, "You wouldn't be telling bad lies yourself, would you now?"

"No. I hear him," she answered simply.

Barney said, "Did you"; and then, in a burst of irritation that was more for himself than the waiting girl: "Well, do you want to tell me about it, or not?"

Confused by direct attack, Marja stammered: "I—I get in trouble, maybe?"

"Why?"

When she did not answer he said, "All right, you better keep it," and turned back to his open door. Marja beat him to it, hands fluttering.

"I like to tell you, Meester Barney, if you don't tell my lady?"

"Mrs. Schafft?" She nodded. "All right, I won't. What's the big lie?"

Marja took a deep breath and a fresh grip on the nearest sleeve, and leaned towards him. "They are to have a divorce, Meester Barney. The policeman ask that, and Meester Theo say 'No.' But that is not true. I know."

"How?"

"I listen always when that lady came here," said Marja frankly. "She talk much, and always beautiful, and laugh too. I like to hear. But this time is no laughing. She talk very serious and sad to Meester Theo, and he is serious too. He says 'No' to her, just like to the policeman, but she still talk. A long, long time."

"What did she say?"

"I don't hear much, she talk so low. So my lady don't hear, I think. But I hear when Meester Theo talk. He don't say much, but I hear."

"You're sure they were talking about a divorce, Marja? You know what that is?"

Marja looked at him with reproach. "I know, yes. I know the names of all great sins. And many little ones," she added coaxingly, widening her grip. Barney dealt with it absently.

"Why didn't you tell this to the policeman, Marja? Didn't he talk to you?"

He wasn't prepared for the fervor of her whispered reply, which was delivered close to his ear, with both arms flung around his neck.

"You tell, Meester Barney! You tell that policeman!"

"Why? You want to get Mr. Theo in trouble?"

She said "Huh?" against his cheek. He unwound the arms, and said it again. Marja considered her position, which was a losing one at the moment, and then his question. Finally she shook her head.

"I like that lady—he must not tell lies about her, so. She is so pretty, Meester Barney. Like you."

A door closed somewhere downstairs. Marja made a quick dash toward Barney's open one, was caught halfway, and grew wide-eyed with terror as someone came into the downstairs hall.

"Go on, Marja—up!"

"Oh, Meester Barney! You tell?"

"No, no, I won't tell."

"Yes, yes! The policeman!"

"All right, then—yes. But get!"

She got, her feet noiseless on the uncovered wooden steps, and Barney was back in his room with the door closed by the time whoever it was got to the landing.

Undressing in the dark, he tried to get rid of obscure guilt feelings. It wasn't so much the encounter with Marja—although he was glad Mrs. Schafft hadn't arrived in the middle of it—as his own meddlesomeness that bothered him. Why hadn't he let the girl hang onto her confounded lie? It was none of his business, and he didn't know what to do with it now he'd got hold of it. He could see himself trailing into Eggart's office the next day, with his secondhand eavesdropping to report—and he could see Marja, subsequently, surrounded by strange faces and hysterically denying everything.

But what difference did the problematical divorce make, even if it was true that Lenore Bellane had wanted it, and Schafft had not? Even if that was what had sent her back to the Clyde to take her life, it wouldn't help anyone, now, to have the fact known.

He lay awake in the dark a long while, hearing the quiet bedtime preparations going on outside his door. Out in the street cars still went by, and slowed, and let anonymous faces peer out. "That's it—that's where the husband lives, and the girl. Imagine! They didn't even know she'd done it till this taxi driver ... And her with another man...."

This taxi driver, Barney thought, had done enough. He'd better stick to his taxi driving, and let the police dig up their own trouble—and the newspapers their own dirt. That was what it would end up in, Lenore's divorce—another paragraph, "Husband Denies Wife Asked for Freedom," and another parade of sightseers tomorrow night. Well, nuts to that. They'd had their money's worth out of Waterford Street and the Schaffts.

But it was a long time before he got to sleep.

Chapter Eleven

Bott wasn't down when Barney went by the office next morning, a copy of the early edition tucked under his arm. Hookey, doodling at his desk, was surly about it.

"He ain't been in or called up, even. Yesterday I ast him was he sick, and he near took my head off. Jeez, is this a taxi company, or what?"

"Sure it is, Hookey. Just don't ask him any more questions for a while."

"Hell, I don't care. I'm no stockholder. Let him run the joint his way—it's his joint."

There was more pride than truth in this, for Hookey was as much a part of the Bottman Taxi Company as the shabby office furniture. It was true that he got little more profit out of it than those venerable relics, plus the same amount of hard usage; but it was the one place in the world where he belonged, and his loyalty to it was a phenomenon of fierceness. Bott's secrets were his secrets—when he could get hold of them.

So without much compunction, Barney tossed his paper over.

"It's all in there, Hook. The name is Schafft, and I don't think Bott feels much like talking about it yet. They're the people he lives with."

Hookey's flat "Yeah?" bore no relation to the immediate lightening of his face, or to the swiftness with which he seized on the paper. Barney left him reading away, and went out to his cab once more.

An hour later, after one thirty-cent fare and forty minutes of gloomy thought, he turned up at police headquarters and asked for Eggart.

The lieutenant did not look much more cheerful than Barney felt. It was Cooney, secure in the possession of the Mystery Man, who had released the Medical Examiner's report on Lenore Bellane's wounds, and released it just about the time Eggart had been holding himself in, in the Schaffts' dining room. Therefore his reply to Barney's first question was curter than usual.

"If you read it in the papers, it must be true. Why? Maybe you want police protection?"

"I'll need it, if I keep on this way. Look, Lieutenant—something turned up last night that's none of my business, and maybe it isn't true anyhow. But if it's a murder case, I guess it's up to you to decide what's true and what isn't."

"That's a nice build-up," said Eggart politely. "What is it—blood in the bathtub?"

"No, it's the maid. The Schaffts' maid. She's afraid of you, so she wants me to pass on something she heard, or says she heard, last Sunday."

"Why you?"

"Because I'm sucker enough to do it, I guess," said Barney grimly. Eggart grinned, and leaned back.

"She doesn't know how you feel about giving other

people's evidence for them, does she? Okay, what is it?"

"She says she heard Mrs. Bellane—or Mrs. Schafft—asking Schafft for a divorce, and he was refusing. She was doing her best to listen, but apparently that's all she heard—Mrs. Schafft asking, and Schafft saying no. Her name's Marja, and she's not very bright, and she may deny the whole thing," he finished. "And for God's sake, don't drag me out to the house with you this time!"

Eggart considered him, and then leaned forward to pick up his pencil.

"I could get her down here. What's her last name?"

"I don't know. She'd probably die of fright on the way."

"What's she so afraid of?"

"Everything, I guess. She's just a kid, from some orphan home."

"She doesn't like the Schaffts?"

"I don't think she has anything against them, but she overheard Schafft talking to you last night, and saying nobody wanted a divorce. She liked Mrs. Bellane, and doesn't want anybody telling lies about her."

"She liked her?"

"She thought she was pretty," said Barney, and felt his face get hot.

Eggart observed this too, but said only: "So you still live there?"

"I did this morning. Maybe my things will be waiting for me in the street when I get home tonight."

"I'll keep you out of it, if I can," Eggart conceded. "It looks like you may be useful out there."

Barney's color, which had started to go down, regained its brilliance. "I hope you're wrong. I'd like to go back to plain taxi driving, after today."

Eggart let him go with amusement and concealed sympathy. Even with years of toughening, he still did not relish a case that brought him, inquisitorial, into the kind of lives that go down fighting to keep their respectability. Luckily there were not many of these. His concern was mainly with unbashful persons who wanted to keep, first, their own lives and liberty, and second, other people's property. He no longer minded taking any of these away from them; but he didn't look forward to seeing the Schaffts' not-overbright maid.

He met with no difficulty. Old Mrs. Schafft turned both Marja and the living room over to him without demur; and Marja's first fear was drowned by the discovery that he meant her no harm and was also, at close range, within her definition of the word "pretty." She readily told him all that she had told Barney on the preceding night; and as if regretful that it was so little, spun it out with wide smiles and even a tentative stroke at his dark sleeve.

He did not have to ask for Schafft when he had finished with Marja. The music teacher was waiting for him, his face pale and his deep eyes bloodshot. He came in to stand braced against Edith's piano, as if drawing strength from its dark beauty, and stammered that the papers—that he had seen in the papers ...

"So you read them now, Mr. Schafft," said Eggart quietly, and was rewarded with a brief display of rage. It was monstrous that the newspapers should be told before Lenore's own family! Why had he said nothing the night before? He must have known—

"Perhaps neither of us was as frank as he should have been," Eggart suggested. "You can't expect frankness when you don't give it."

Schafft was suddenly quiet, and no longer angry.

What did the lieutenant mean? Eggart said his information was that Mrs. Schafft had asked for a divorce that Sunday afternoon, and watched Schafft round the piano to sit heavily on its bench.

"I suppose you mean Marja. It's all right. I should have told you myself, if you hadn't let me believe Lenore took her own life. It could have made no difference then, except to hurt Edith. To hurt all of us—and Lenore herself, her memory—"

"Then it's true?"

"It's true that she spoke to me about a divorce. I didn't believe then—I don't believe now she would have gone through with it, if I had agreed. Why should she have wanted one?"

"She gave you no reason?"

"No real reason. That was why I was so sure it was an emotional impulse on her part—something she would regret later."

"But she spent a long time, trying to persuade you."

"Was it a long time? It didn't seem—I don't remember that it was. It makes no difference."

"You and Mrs. Schafft were alone then?"

"Oh, yes—in the dining room. It was after dinner, about three."

"Did any of the others know what you and your wife were discussing?"

"No, none of them. I—I still haven't told them. Why should they know? Why should anyone ..." He stopped, and brought his great hands together on the closed piano lid.

"Why were you opposed to a divorce, Mr. Schafft?"

"Why? Does it concern you? Yes—all right; I suppose it does. I don't believe in divorce, sir. It's not a religious scruple—you might call it a philosophical one. We were both mature and earnest when we made this contract—it wasn't one to be dissolved simply by legal agreement—or even private agreement. Not unless our consciences were dissolved at the same time."

"Yet Mrs. Schafft was divorced before she married you?"

"That was entirely different. The circumstances were tragic, and there was no real marriage there in the first place. A legal one, yes; but hasty, and foolish."

"But there was a child."

"Edith, yes. Poor little Edith." He looked down at the piano with despairing eyes, as if it were she. "What effect all this will have on her ... nothing can be worth it. A true artist is not like other people, Lieutenant."

"What arrangement did Mrs. Schafft propose for her daughter, after the divorce?"

"We did not discuss that."

"Didn't you ask her what her plans were?"

"Of course not!" Schafft exclaimed with sudden restlessness. "We weren't having a rational discussion of rational plans, don't you understand that? At the time, I could hardly believe my ears—now I realize that I misjudged Lenore, that this wasn't her doing at all. It was those Bellanes! They've been a curse to her from the very beginning."

"Did your wife mention Bellane?"

"No. If she had, I should have realized."

"Realized what?"

"That she wasn't acting under her own initiative, clearly."

"Do you have any idea why Bellane should have urged her to get a divorce?"

"Edith, I suppose. They have been willing to let her starve, or run the streets, for years. Now that she has turned out to be an unusual child—a credit to anyone—they remember that her name is Bellane, too."

"You say 'they,' Mr. Schafft. Who?"

"Bellane has a wife, I know. An invalid, and I believe extremely wealthy. They have no children of their own, and they may think they have some right to their brother's neglected child. Now that they choose to exercise that right," he added scornfully.

"Do you have any reason to think they actually were planning to take Edith under their protection?"

Schafft shrugged. "What else can explain Lenore's behavior? She would never have taken such a course of her own accord—never!"

"Did Mrs. Schafft have legal advice? Do you know her lawyers?"

"Lawyers? Lenore had no lawyers."

"Didn't her daughter's allowance come through some legal firm? Who were they?"

Schafft hesitated, and a curious expression—half surprise and half dismay—came over his face. After a moment he muttered, "Edith has never used any of that money. Every penny of it can be given back. Every penny."

"Do you remember the name of the firm?"

Schafft did not. He got up and went, with his slow, shambling gait, through the portieres to the dining room. Eggart could hear him calling his mother, and her low reply from the back of the house. There was a brief delay, and then Schafft returned with a half sheet of notepaper, which he gave to Eggart. On it was written, in the careful, rather childlike hand of old age, "Weatherby, Weatherby and Long, New York."

"Thanks," Eggart said, folding it and putting it away. "Now may I see Miss Bellane?"

"She isn't—she's not at home."

"When will she be back?"

"Why, I can't say for certain."

"You know where she is, I suppose."

"She's staying with Mr. Bottman's mother for the present," said Schafft, helplessly. "The newspapers ... I can't give you the exact address."

"Perhaps you could get it for me."

With a suggestion of defeat in his large, stooping body, Schafft went once more in search of his mother and presently returned with what looked like the other half of the sheet of notepaper. Eggart thanked him gravely and pocketed this, too. Schafft, once more reduced to gloomy silence, let him out the door; there was no sign of old Mrs. Schafft, or the friendly Marja.

In his car once more, Eggart hesitated with his hand on the ignition key, wondering which of three interviews should take precedence. As he did so, a non-Bottman taxi cut in behind him, came to a stop, and put an end to his indecision. Francis Bellane, hatless and elegant, got out of the back.

Eggart put his head out of the window and hailed him; and Bellane, eyebrows raised, came down the edge of the lawn towards him. Eggart opened the car door. "Mind getting in a minute, Mr. Bellane?"

Bellane bent his long body and complied, smiling faintly. In the morning sunlight his pale skin had a slight yellowish tinge, and the ruined setting for his fine eyes was more than ever apparent. Nevertheless he was a good-looking man, sitting there easily at Eggart's side, with the door open beside him.

"I'm on my way to see Edith. You said that would be all right, I think?"

"It's all right with me. There are a couple of things I want to talk to you about first."

"Anything at all."

"The main thing is that you'd be wise in correcting yesterday's statement. Mrs. Schafft was here to ask for a divorce; it's no secret, and no one in the world is going to believe that you didn't know it—you, who came all the way up here to help her out. Frankly, I can't even see your purpose in trying to keep it quiet."

"I'm not trying to keep anything quiet—God forbid! But you mean she actually asked for it? Sunday?"

"Come off it, Mr. Bellane."

"No, really, Lieutenant! I can hardly believe it. Why, that divorce has been a standing joke for years—I never dreamed she'd get up the nerve to actually— Does Schafft say it's true?"

"This isn't doing you any good, you know. It's a lot better to change your statement now, voluntarily, than to make us dig the truth out somewhere else. Which we will."

The heavy brows drew into a straight line, and Eggart watched them with interest.

"You can check everything I've said to you as thoroughly as you like. You won't find any contradictions."

Without shifting his scrutiny Eggart said, "You're a widower?"

"Yes."

"When did your wife die?"

"Quite recently—and quite normally. Be sure to check that, too."

"How recently?"

"This past month; she had been in poor health for years. I suppose all this is relevant?"

"You know that as well as I do," said Eggart. "That's all, for now. I wouldn't try to leave Boston, if I were you."

"Why not?" Bellane inquired, without moving, "You're full of vague threats this morning, my friend."

"It's neither vague nor a threat. I'm telling you that if you try to leave town, you won't get far. That's simple information, Mr. Bellane. The kind you can prove by testing it."

"Perhaps I'll do that," said Bellane, his full lips pale with anger. He got out, slamming the door at his back, and started up the walk. The taxi behind Eggart's car had driven off, and he turned and went back down the street, passing another taxi drawn in beside the curb.

Abreast of this he slowed down, put his head out, and said to the solitary passenger: "You won't have to wait long—he should be right out. And stick to him like a brother!"

Then, leaving Edith and Bott till later, he went directly back to his own office for an interview with Cooney that changed his plans for the rest of the day and some time to follow.

Chapter Twelve

The rest of the day, following his interview with Eggart, was confused and not pleasant for Barney.

While his conscience was still heavy, Bott buttonholed him in the office for a long discussion of the morning's news, which turned out to be, mainly, a monologue by Bott. That Lenore's death was no suicide, he said, he had known from the minute he heard the details; but seeing the official confirmation in print had excited him to further reminiscence and pronouncements—mainly about Francis Bellane.

"They're no good, those Bellanes," he told Barney solemnly. "Here, Hookey—run over and get us some coffee, will you? And don't be so damn' quick about it." Hookey caught the coin, winked at Barney, and disappeared. "They're one of these old families—played out.

Edith's got new blood in her, but those two Bellane brothers—well, they're the kind that's played out before they begin. Big ideas, and no money left to back 'em, and don't know any way to get money but marry it...."

It was nearly an hour before Barney escaped; and then his freedom did not last long. Late in the afternoon Bott wanted him back again, and he returned fully prepared to hand in his cap and card and find another job for the month that remained before school opened. But Bott was still innocent of the treachery within his gates; all he wanted was a driver to take him over to his mother's house, after Edith.

Barney waited a long time there, in front of the small, story-and-a-half frame house with its sloping porch and decaying steps. All the houses on the street were built to much the same pattern, and worn to the same degree. Barney wondered which had been Lenore's, and what could have brought her back from New York and her "social" young husband to this shabby obscurity.

When Bott reappeared, Edith was with him. A pronounced difference in her appearance made Barney look at her sharply until he realized that it was her hair. Gone was the neat, intricate arrangement of braids, evidently old Mrs. Schafft's work; the masses of dark hair were loosely caught back in a low knot, making her seem both softer and more mature.

She looked tired and dispirited, too, but her temper was even as always. To Bott's eager, half-placative attempts at conversation she kept up low-voiced replies; he seemed pleased that she recognized Barney and said "Hello" to him.

"Edith's going over to the house a while," he explained. "Wants to get some of her music, and stuff.

Maybe we'll stay for dinner—would you like that, honey?"

She would, and it was settled. From Bott's remarks, made in his usual hearty, carrying voice, Barney gathered that both he and Edith had had a visit from Eggart during the afternoon; but neither Marja nor a divorce was mentioned, and Barney gave mental thanks to the lieutenant for his discretion.

Schafft let them in, and revived a little under Edith's kiss.

"There's a piano over there, Uncle Theo. It's an old player, but I thought I could just fool with it."

"That's right, dear," he answered automatically. "An idle day requires two of practice.... What have you done to your hair, child?"

Old Mrs. Schafft appeared from her room, which was on the first floor somewhere at the back, and the hall began to seem crowded. Barney made an attempt to get out the front door, and was stopped by Bott.

"You better hang around, feller—be ready to take us back. Tell you what, why don't you have supper with us? Marthe, got enough food for one more?"

She said calmly that there was plenty for everyone, and Barney's hasty disclaimer was generally ignored. Mainly to get out of the way, he went upstairs to wash, and have a cigarette in his room. Bott found him there presently, and brought him down to the dinner table.

It was the first time he had been in the back of the house. The dining room lay behind the living room, and was adjoined on one side by old Mrs. Schafft's bedroom, to which the door stood open. It was a large, old-fashioned room, with a round table heavily furnished with linens and old china and silver. To Barney, long accustomed to perfunctory restaurant service, it looked extremely pleasant, and old Mrs. Schafft told

him where to sit with no apparent horror and dismay.
Schafft, preparing to mumble grace, paused to wish
him good evening, and Edith sent him a little smile
across the table. He began to feel less like a skeleton
at the feast, and his exasperation with Bott died down.

But the dinner was not a pleasant meal after all,
and before it was over Edith had left the table in tears,
Bott and Schafft had gotten into a clash, and Schafft
and his mother into another. And some of this, at least,
was Barney's doing.

It began with Bott's attempts to keep conversation
going. No one else was much disposed to talk, and he
gradually drifted into a monologue. He was talking
about Lieutenant Eggart, and approvingly. Bott himself could find no fault in the way he had behaved toward Edith that afternoon.

"But he's no softy—he knows his job, and he'll do it.
He's more than a match for Bellane, let me tell you—
just the fellow to handle a smooth talker like him.
Eggart'll just let him soft-soap himself into a regular
lather, and then dunk him in cold water. He won't
know what hit him."

"Uncle Francis doesn't soft-soap people," Edith protested. "He's just naturally polite, Bott."

"You don't know anything about him, Edith. Anybody
seems nice that just takes you out to dinner now and
then."

"But you don't know as much about him as I do,
Bott! He really is nice—it's not just pretending."

"Edith, honey, when you've had as much experience
at sizing people up as I have, you don't get fooled.
You're a little girl, and a sweet one, and you couldn't
be expected to see black hearts under white shirts.
You take it from your old Bott—"

Edith put down her spoon, and Schafft interposed.

"We're none of us in a position to judge this man, Bott, and there's no use upsetting Edith."

"Yes, there is," said Bott obstinately. "I don't mean to upset her, but the longer she goes on idealizing this fellow—"

"Oh, Bott! I'm not idealizing anyone! It's just that—"

"It's just that he's got you fooled, Edith, and it's not your fault. I'm not blaming you. But just stop and ask yourself what he ever did for you—your own flesh and blood. Anybody can be pleasant a couple of evenings, but did he offer to help your mother when you were little and she was having such a hard time? Did he ever do one thing for you that put him out the least bit? Why, he never even took you to his house! Entertaining you in restaurants, like he was ashamed of you!"

"He wasn't ashamed of us! It was just that Aunt Sandra was sick—"

"He says! She wasn't too sick to say hello to a little girl—don't tell me. 'Aunt Sandra!' Why, she never even saw you—never sent you so much as a birthday card. You have to learn to think these things out, Edith, and not be taken in by a big smile, and somebody saying 'Call me Uncle.' He's no real uncle to you, honey, and never has been. What do you think would have happened if you had gone to him and said, 'Uncle Francis [Here Bott produced a horrible falsetto] I need a new piano, and it's only three thousand dollars.' 'What do you think would have happened to that big smile then?"

Edith, her face as pale as Barney's was scarlet, put down her napkin and twisted out of her chair. Bott's face, hard with the intensity of his argument, grew slack with surprise. He tried to push his own chair back, but she was out of the room before he got free;

and from the hopeless sound of his voice in the hall, Barney guessed that she had left the stairs before he reached them.

"You haven't taken any peas, Mr. Chance," observed Mrs. Schafft, and gave him the dish. He got four or five on his plate and one on the tablecloth, and then Bott came back, crumpling his napkin in one big paw.

"Oh, God, why don't I keep my big mouth shut?" he groaned. "I never meant to … But it shows you, Theo, the way this guy has got under her skin! You just can't let a helpless little girl go along blind, and then suddenly find out what he's really like—what he's done!"

Nobody answered, and Bott sat down heavily.

"Everything I said was true—you know that, Theo. Marthe, did I say one thing that wasn't true?"

"It's not what you say, Edward. It's the way you say it."

Bott, relieved at having got an answer, began to defend himself. "Well, I'm rough, and I know it—Edith knows it. She knows I'm no Harvard graduate, but she does know—"

"She does know that you bought her piano, and paid three thousand dollars for it," Schafft interrupted, his voice trembling. "And in case it ever slips her mind, you'll be sure to remind her again."

Bott stared, and then his eyes narrowed. He leaned over his plate, and said emphatically, "So is that something to be afraid to talk about? She was never ashamed of my getting it for her before—why should she be now? She knows every damn' thing I got in the world is hers, don't she? She knows who sends her to the Conservatory, don't she?"

Barney put his napkin down, too.

"I'm going out and close the cab windows—it looks

like rain. Excuse me."

He took a determined walk through the quiet living room and hall, out into the tranquil evening sunshine, and sat in the cab long enough to run up glass barriers against the beginning breeze. Then, although the temptation to start the car in motion and go anywhere in it was enormous, he went indoors again and took his place at the table. Schafft gave him a brief, rather nervous smile, but neither of the other two so much as looked up. The whole situation was so far outside the bounds of normal behavior that his intense embarrassment suddenly disappeared. Obviously no one but Schafft cared what he thought, anyway; old Mrs. Schafft was imperturbable, and Bott sunk in gloom; and Schafft's perceptions of the outer world were so vague and fleeting at all times that he had forgotten Barney before he got his napkin spread.

The silence continued; it began to make Barney a little lightheaded. He found himself asking, after one of Mrs. Schafft's frequent trips to the kitchen, if Marja wasn't well? No part of the ceiling fell on him, and nobody but Mrs. Schafft took any notice of the question. She replied that, so far as she knew, Marja was perfectly all right.

About three minutes later Schafft lifted his head and asked where she was.

"I've sent her away," his mother replied tranquilly.

"Away where?" Schafft demanded, looking like a man wakened from heavy sleep.

"Back where she came from."

"To St. Vincent's? Good heavens, mother—you've never done such a thing!"

"Why not?"

"Why not? To send her back there now, of all times!"

"I don't follow you, Theodore. The time when Marja

proves herself unsatisfactory seems to me the time to send her away."

Schafft took a firm grip of his fork, as if it were the point in question. "You had no right to punish the girl for doing what she thought was her duty, mother! Perhaps she should have come to one of us first, but she was an unfortunate child—she shouldn't be judged like a normal one. Besides, I should infinitely prefer to have her here than chattering about our affairs to strangers!"

"Our affairs are already public property, son. And I am not punishing Marja. It is simply that I will not have a servant who listens to private conversations."

Bott looked indifferently at the dish of sliced peaches which she placed before him, and then stood up.

"I think I'll take these up to Edith," he mumbled. "She always likes fresh peaches ..."

"I'd leave her alone, Bott," said Schafft; but Bott paid no attention and presently shambled out of the room, bearing the fragile dish carefully. Schafft turned back to his mother with renewed earnestness.

"Mother, I feel very strongly about this. Marja was a good, hard-working girl. She may be in trouble with the people at the home over this, and she doesn't deserve it. I think you should take her back."

"I don't try to choose your pupils, son—you must let me choose my own maid. Marja won't get into any trouble, and she'll soon find another place."

"But did you tell them why you were sending her away?"

"I did not."

Schafft hesitated, the forcefulness of his first protest seeping away, and only vague dissatisfaction remaining in its place.

"Did you tell Marja?"

"Marja had no need to be told, Theodore. She knows quite well that eavesdropping is wrong."

The peaches in Barney's dish were excellent, and neatly peeled and cut up to bite-size; but he had no appetite for them. Neither had Schafft, nor—evidently—Edith, since Bott soon returned with his little peace offering and put it back on the table without a word.

Altogether, the dinner party broke up in low spirits. Bott went upstairs once more, and Schafft into the music parlor. Barney, his offer to help Mrs. Schafft clear away refused, ended up in his own room, alone. Here he waited till past nine o'clock, but no instructions came from behind Bott's closed door; finally he went down and locked up the cab for the night.

He stayed dressed a little longer, just in case, and then gave up and went to bed. A few slow bars of piano music drifted up to him as he lay there, but he did not know whether it was Schafft playing, or Edith; and the music died away before he could decide.

Chapter Thirteen

The next morning found Eggart in New York with Cooney's blessing, but not altogether at ease with himself. Ostensibly his purpose was to follow Francis Bellane's affairs behind the curtain of bland information which Bellane himself had drawn over them; and behind that curtain, Eggart knew, Cooney hoped to find a strong enough motive to bring Bellane down. Eggart had left his superior happily spreading out nets to catch the car or plane Bellane had used on his furtive return trip to Boston, late Sunday night; that there was such a car or plane Cooney no more doubted than he doubted Eggart's existence.

The lieutenant wished him well, and envied him his cheerful certainty. He himself meant to carry out Cooney's orders implicitly, and to examine every aspect of Francis Bellane's past and present; but he was afraid that the information he got would be a beginning, more than an end, and that Lenore Bellane's affairs were more complicated than even she had known—until the last minute, perhaps.

It was Edith who intrigued him most. Everywhere he turned in this case, he ran up against the girl. In herself she seemed harmless enough and even pathetic, but she was the only clear trail Lenore Bellane had left behind her, the only apparent link with the queer, indifferent people who had been Lenore Bellane's family and friends. His first exasperation with the girl's ubiquity had begun to turn into interest. With no definite end in view but a general clearing up of the situation, he had spent the previous evening in making a list of all the motives the daughter gave for her mother's death.

Bellane he left in abeyance. That link was not yet clear, although he believed that it existed. But between Theodore Schafft and his wandering wife, the only connection Eggart could see was Edith.

He had had Schafft's history turned up, and found it a quiet one. He was the son of a fairly successful doctor, and had been a kind of prodigy in his youth. Before Schafft was twenty he had appeared as soloist with several of the smaller symphony orchestras, and had even played a Fantasy for Piano and Orchestra that he had composed. After his father's death, when Schafft was twenty-one, he had begun giving music lessons to help out at home; the doctor's estate had been a small one, and most of it was needed to keep up the house. From here on, there was almost no trace of the young musician. Whether his early talent had petered out, or been smothered in financial cares, or whether it had never been strong enough to compete in such a narrow, overcrowded field, there was no one to say. He gave an occasional recital over local radio stations, sometimes playing his own work; the Fantasy had one more performance, by someone else, out of town. That was about all.

As a piano teacher he had an excellent reputation for "bringing out" talented children, but when the children began to think of the piano as a career, or a serious accomplishment, they went on to study elsewhere. Edith was a case in point. She had been studying lately at the Conservatory, where there was considerable enthusiasm about her. No one doubted that she would make a career for herself, under the proper conditions. What would this mean to Schafft, the one-time prodigy?

It was true he no longer taught her, but she was his discovery, and developing under his care and protection. Did he see in her another chance at that lost world of music, with this girl who was almost his own child? And how far would he go to keep that chance, and that child? Eggart thought he had put up with a lot so far to keep her: Lenore's whims, and the humiliation of her long absence, and the presence of Bott in Schafft's home.

In spite of Bott's easy air with his host, Eggart couldn't see them as bosom friends. There was too much difference in the two men. No, the link was Lenore—and Edith. Bott's money was necessary for Edith's career, and Bott's presence was necessary for that reason. And it would probably take a stronger man than Schafft to dislodge the old taxi driver, anyway, after so many years.

This paternal aspect of Mr. Edward J. Bottman fascinated Eggart. For years that hard, red-faced man had been one of the familiar, accepted facets of the local scene. You ran across him in obscure restaurants where the tablecloths were soiled and the food lavish; you brushed up against him at prizefights and baseball games; you were aware of him as a well-heeled old bachelor, hard as granite, aggressively law-abiding; a "character," in short. He was like an old-time hotel you had never been in, and yet spoke of with slightly contemptuous affection. If it were pulled down, you went by the vacant space with a sense of shock.

And yet all the time he had had this secret core of family life, this purpose no one had guessed, and yet which seemed to occupy all his private energy. For the first time Bott lost his faintly humorous aspect. Such a man, with such a fixation, was something Eggart could not wholly understand; but he could respect the fact that this new Bott was different, and might even be dangerous.

The old lady was harder to make out. Eggart still was not sure what her relations with her adopted granddaughter were. They seemed to be cordial; they might even be affectionate, although he suspected that with her, Schafft came first every time. But as a person she, too, was someone to be reckoned with. She might be in her seventies, but she was still firm, erect, intelligent—even, Eggart thought, quite strong. What her son wanted, she would want, and she looked as though her purpose would be firmer than Schafft's. Except that it was hard to gauge a man like the music teacher, when most of him, like an iceberg, seemed to be below surface. Well, there were the four of them, at any rate. Bellane, Schafft, Bott, and old Mrs. Schafft.

So far no one else connected with the dead woman had turned up. The first husband was alive, but had been out of touch with her for years—was remarried, and off at a summer camp in Maine. The cosmetic house of Princess Natasha presented an impersonal, if horrified, front to the whole affair. He made a reluctant note to call on the princess, and settled back to wait for the end of his journey.

As soon as his train got in he had breakfast at the station, and took the subway down to Centre Street. His particular friend, an inspector who had known his father, was waiting with some of the information Eggart had sent ahead for. It was routine background on Francis Bellane and his wife, who had been Sandra Congrave, a paper heiress from St. Louis. Bellane had brought his delicate wife and her sturdy bank account to New York nearly twenty-five years ago, and spent the intervening years very peacefully with them, at first in Manhattan and later on Long Island. His stock-broking activities, if not spectacular, were at least bona fide. There had been one incident some years back when Bellane had been unwise enough to handle stock in a corporation that had just lost its government sanctions; but since there was no proof of intent to defraud, and since Mrs. Bellane had come vigorously to her husband's aid, the whole affair had been dropped.

The two Bellane boys, while impeccably bred and schooled, had had no fortune of their own. Paul, the elder, had become an architect and a successful one; Francis had taken refuge in Miss Congrave and a genteel connection on Wall Street. Since his wife's death, the preceding month, he had become very close to a millionaire in his own right.

Mrs. Bellane's death had not only been perfectly natural, but long overdue. Her doctor had been surprised at the ailing lady's ability to hang on so long, and was perfectly certain that no one had hurried her on her eventual way.

Eggart wasn't discouraged by all this respectability. It was much what he had expected, and thanks to his friend the inspector's competence had taken very little of his morning. By ten-thirty he was free to go back uptown to the offices of Weatherby, Weatherby & Long.

A very young Mr. Weatherby saw him almost at once, and was pleasant, if alert. He had read of Mrs. Bellane-Schafft's death, and was sorry, although he had never met the lady.

"You've never transacted any business for her?"

"None at all."

"Would you be able to tell me if there was any prospect that you would be acting for her? I mean, had there been any discussion about it?"

"Not with us," said young Weatherby good-humoredly. "If she was doing legal business, I'm afraid it was somewhere else. And I can't tell you where, because I don't know."

"But you are her ex-husband's lawyer?"

"You've got the wrong Bellane. That's Paul. The only member of the family we act for is Francis Bellane."

"You don't handle the elder brother's business at all? You never have?"

"Never have," Weatherby agreed. "Sorry I can't be more helpful."

Just how helpful he had been, Eggart thought it better not to mention then. If Weatherby, Weatherby & Long did not act for Paul Bellane, then it was not Paul Bellane who sent those monthly checks to Edith. And from what Eggart had seen of Francis, he did not think he would be doing good by stealth without a reason.

Well satisfied with the interview, Eggart went farther uptown and invaded the fragrant domain of Princess Natasha. Any one of the lovely, lacquered young women through whose well-manicured hands he passed might have posed for portraits of Her Highness without straining belief; but he was oddly relieved to find the inner sanctum occupied by a brisk, middle-aged woman named Mrs. Sebold. Mrs. Sebold's shrewd eyes measured him through their own scanty lashes, and her smile was no less pleasant because it revealed frank wrinkles.

She said, "You're a new one, aren't you? Why do they keep sending you fellows up here? I can't tell you a damned thing more about that poor woman. You probably know more about her right now than we do."

"She was with you for nearly eight years, wasn't she?"

"With us, but not of us," said Mrs. Sebold cheerfully. "Mind you, she was good at her work—she wouldn't have lasted so long otherwise, Bellane or no Bellane. But we didn't know she had either a husband or a daughter until we read about them in the newspapers. That'll give you an idea."

"She didn't say much about herself?"

"Yes, she did. Frankly, she could talk your ear off, and all on the same subject. I always thought her a lonely, rather self-centered woman with too much time to think about herself—and all the time she was sitting on this volcano, whatever it is. Goes to show."

"Didn't she ever mention any friends—any social life?"

"Just my brother Francis," said Mrs. Sebold, with a grin. "We heard a lot about my brother Francis. I'm afraid we took it all with a grain of salt."

"What would she say about Mr. Bellane?"

"Nothing important. Nothing to remember. Just little reminders that she was *au mieux* with our heavy stockholder—all very sweet, of course."

"She wasn't popular?"

Mrs. Sebold hesitated. "Popular? Well, I don't know. She wasn't unpopular, and she certainly got along with her clients. The thing is that she'd come to be rather a joke, I'm sorry to say, among the rest of us. Just too perfectly ladylike, and all that. The girls used to call her Princess Natasha, behind her back."

"She hadn't any particular friend here?"

"No, I'm quite certain she hadn't. Nor enemies either, which is rather unusual in a hothouse full of women. She managed to keep away from both extremes, which is enough in itself to prove she was no fool, I suppose."

"In other words, then, she was getting along smoothly here?"

"Perfectly. And at home, too, so far as we knew."

Eggart then asked about the beginning of Lenore's connection with the firm, about Bellane's patronage and how far it went, and made sure that she had had no reason connected with Princess Natasha for being in Boston the past weekend. He went away finally not much wiser than he had come, but still not dissatisfied. His passion for details was insatiable; and since it had produced more than one good result for him in the past, he gave it rein whenever he could.

After a hasty luncheon in a midtown cafeteria he took the bus down Fifth Avenue, got off at Twelfth Street, and walked nearly to Sixth Avenue examining numbers. Lenore Bellane's apartment was in one of the narrow, four-story ex-residences which are so common in the neighborhood. Its red brick façade was not so lovingly decorated with window boxes, shutters, and whitewash as some of its neighbors, but neither was it shabby. The little entrance hall displayed an incredible number of letter boxes, and the caretaker emerged from the first-floor-back still chewing his lunch. Eggart displayed his credentials, and was taken up three flights of carpeted stair to a door at the back of the house which still carried a neatly printed card: "Mrs. Lenore Bellane."

The apartment itself consisted of one large, chintz-and-maple room with a bed disguised as a divan, a built-in kitchenette, and a small tiled bath. Nothing, the caretaker said, had been disturbed or taken away, even though the police had been there once.

Looking around him, before he touched a thing, Eggart was struck by a sudden feeling of pity for the woman who had lived here. The room, although pleasant, was much as the decorator had left it; and that was strange, for a woman as feminine and personal as Lenore Bellane. It was as if she had regarded this home of hers as she might have done a hotel room: something temporary, and no part of herself. And yet, the caretaker said, she had lived here nearly two years. He began to realize that he was dealing with a woman who had lived almost entirely in her own mind, and in her hope for the future. Everything real in her life—her husband and daughter, her job, her home—she seemed to have regarded as a compromise with the present, something temporary that would be rearranged when her real life began. Only the future was real, for Lenore Bellane. But it was the present— or the past—that had killed her.

There was not even a radio in the apartment. A few fashion magazines were piled in the bookcase, and several recently issued novels, in their jackets, that opened with the stiffness of unread books. Presents, Eggart thought, and looked at all the flyleaves carefully. There was nothing written on them.

Her wardrobe was unexpectedly lavish, and well cared for. The dresses hung in cellophane bags, the hats sat in little transparent boxes; the drawers of the lowboy were piled with fragile lingerie, much of it unworn. The general effect was that of a trousseau.

It was in one of these drawers, buried in silk, that he made his only discovery. This was a leather folder, dark green and tooled in gold, that opened to display three studio portraits. One of Lenore, graciously posed in the fashions of the 1920's. The center one of a little girl, her dark hair plaited, seated at a piano. The last a young man with heavy dark hair and eyebrows, his head tilted at an artistic angle, and his large dark eyes looking quizzically into the camera. If it wasn't Francis Bellane, Eggart told himself with grim humor, it was his brother.

Nothing else turned up that he cared to take away with him, although he went through Lenore's desk thoroughly. Her canceled checks and stubs, kept for the past three years, showed that she was of a careful, if not economical, disposition. The balance ran along uniformly, renewing itself in the same amounts at regular intervals; there were no large jumps, or drafts. Apparently she had lived on her salary, and on her salary only.

Edith's letters filled almost an entire, good-sized drawer. Something in the way they were filed away, with dates and rubber bands, reminded him of the banking files. As if the letters, too, were a kind of receipt, or guarantee.

He took out a few recent ones and glanced through them. As Bott had intimated, the correspondence had not been a very confidential one. The girl wrote affectionately, with many small details of her daily life,

but there was no hint of secret understandings between mother and daughter. Anyone might have read
the letters, without offense or jealousy. Eggart wondered if anyone had, besides Lenore.

Late in the afternoon he locked the door behind him
and went downstairs to return the key. The caretaker
was voluble about the approaching month's end, and
the chances of getting the apartment ready to rent.
Eggart told him someone from the dead woman's family would probably show up soon, to take her things
away, and as he spoke he wondered who it would be.
Mrs. Schafft, perhaps, acting on her son's behalf, and
handling those piles of intimate things with silent
disapproval. Or Bellane's housekeeper, making up
bundles for charity, with a weather eye out for herself
and family.

Poor Princess Natasha, he thought, walking up toward the subway entrance on Fourteenth Street. Got
off on the wrong foot, and hopped right along on it, all
the way. Been better for her if she'd never seen the
Royal Brothers.

Feeling out of sympathy with the Bellane boys, he
went back down to Centre Street and took his father's
friend uptown to dinner. Later he caught the night
train to Maine.

Chapter Fourteen

Paul Bellane's summer retreat was a plain, rather
weather-beaten farmhouse some thirty miles from
Bangor. The surrounding countryside, while honest
and fairly prosperous farmland, was clearly no ortho-
dox vacation spot. Eggart asked the local law officer,
who was driving him out in a comfortable sedan, if

Bellane was a regular summer visitor.

"Yep. Been comin' here reg'lar ever since they was married. Wife's a local girl—keeps on her folks' old place fer summers."

So Paul Bellane had evidently gone right on ignoring his brother's example, and marrying daughters of the people. Eggart hoped he had had better luck this time, and thought perhaps he had, after a few minutes' conversation with the present Mrs. Bellane. She was a thin, energetic-looking woman in dungarees, her brown hair cropped like that of her ten-year-old son, and with the same frank manner. Bellane himself was down in the woodlot, she told them, and sent the boy off to find him. Meanwhile, perhaps Mr. Emerson and his friend would like a cup of coffee?

They had come in through the kitchen door, and remained in that wide, happily chaotic room. Eggart found himself, a little self-conscious in his neat dark suit, joining the other two at a large round table, and accepting steaming coffee in a mug. Mrs. Bellane, incurious and hospitable, kept up amiable exchanges with Mr. Emerson and asked for no explanation of Eggart's business. He began wondering how he was going to introduce Lenore Bellane into this company.

However, the matter settled itself. Bellane came in the screen door, a tall, quiet man with intelligent grey eyes and thinning brown hair, detached his strange guest from the coffee-drinkers, and led him back through the house to a kind of den. From his manner Eggart could not tell whether or not he had guessed at the Boston police officer's business; Bellane was polite and noncommittal, settling the lieutenant in an old leather chair and closing the door into the hall, but making no effort to discover what his business was. Eggart, curious to see how long this would go on, said he was sorry to intrude on their vacation.

"It's no intrusion, Mr. Eggart. As a matter of fact, I've been wondering whether or not I should go down to Boston. I decided not to, because there was nothing for me to do there."

"Then you know of your first wife's death?"

"Naturally. No one is completely cut off from the world who has a radio, and listens to the news."

"May I ask whether you've communicated with any-one since you heard?"

"You mean my brother, I suppose," said Bellane, drawing on his pipe. "No, not yet."

"As a matter of fact, I meant your daughter." Bellane's eyes came up to meet his, and then went down.

"I don't believe Edith has any particular need of me, Mr. Eggart. I suppose you've seen her."

"Oh, yes."

"How is she taking it?"

"Pretty hard, Mr. Bellane."

"She was fond of Lenore, then?"

"I should judge so."

"And of Francis?"

"Apparently. She looks on him as her uncle, of course."

This time Bellane removed the pipe from his mouth, and leaned forward a little, frowning. "You're rather an unusual police officer, aren't you?"

"No, pretty usual. Why?"

"I think I might have come down to Boston after all, if I'd known I would be dealing with you. You see, the little I have to contribute could do as much harm as good, depending on the way it was received. I wasn't sure how frank Francis had been with you, nor even whether I would be allowed to see him or not."

"When you say harm, and good, you mean from your

brother's standpoint?"

"Naturally. Whether it's by accident or someone's plan, he's in a very awkward spot. Anything I can do to help, I will do, gladly."

"You and your brother are on good terms, then?"

"Oh, yes. Not close, perhaps; but there's no constraint."

"Isn't that a little unusual, Mr. Bellane?"

"I don't think so. Neither Lenore nor Francis has been particularly fortunate. If they were foolish, at least they paid for their own foolishness." There was no hint of satisfaction in his voice, only a measured gravity, as if he were speaking of people much younger than himself. And yet he was not far over the fifty mark, and might have passed for less. Eggart watched him curiously, and said: "I'd like to hear the whole story from your point of view, Mr. Bellane. You don't seem to have any prejudice one way or the other."

"And Francis has?"

"He's not so detached about it as you. That's natural."

"May I ask if he's under any form of arrest?"

"No, he's staying at a hotel. You might have seen him any time you liked."

"I know news accounts are always wrongly emphasized.... Still, I understood he was back in New York when she died. I don't see why there's any suggestion—"

"Police mills grind pretty slowly, Mr. Bellane. In a case like this everything is checked thoroughly before it's given up, and the checking can't be kept as private as we'd like."

To his relief Bellane seemed satisfied. He settled back in his chair again and resumed his pipe.

"Well, you seem to know the main story. What is it you want me to tell you?"

"The details of the divorce, for one thing. Whose idea was it?"

"It wasn't anyone's 'idea.' It was just the only thing to be done. If you mean did I let Lenore divorce me, yes, I did. She deserved that, for being so completely honest with me, and besides I thought she had enough trouble ahead of her without my adding to it."

"What kind of trouble?"

"With Francis. Don't misunderstand me—I believe he was genuinely fond of her. If he had been free, I'm sure he would have married her. But he wasn't free, and I think Lenore's determination to have everything public, immediately, more or less frightened him. Sandra was well-to-do, and he'd slid into a way of living that he wouldn't have, otherwise, I suppose. At that time I don't think he could have supported Lenore and the baby."

"Did he ask his wife for a divorce?"

Bellane hesitated. "Yes, I'm sure he must have. I did wonder, when Lenore and the baby went back to Boston, what sort of agreement they'd come to. But I wasn't quite as open-minded about the whole thing as I am now, you can understand, and I certainly wasn't in communication with any of them."

"Do you know how things stood at that time?"

"Not precisely, no. I heard from Lenore, once or twice, after she'd been in Boston a year or so. She was rather bitter about Sandra, and seemed to feel that everything was her fault. She wanted me to speak to her. I refused."

"Did you see her after she came back to New York?"

"No, I never ran into her. I saw Francis now and then, and he told me Lenore had a good position, and had married again. He didn't seem pleased about the marriage, and said he didn't think it would last. I had a boy of my own by then, and he used to talk to me about Edith when he saw I had no feeling about what had happened. He was rather hurt at being cast as an uncle, but he could see there was no other way of playing it. In fact, I had the impression they were on excellent terms."

"Was it Bellane's idea that she should stay in New York?"

"No, primarily it was Lenore's. She never got over Francis, you see. Even the child came second. I think she felt safer right there on the spot, where she could keep in touch with him and keep up his interest in Edith."

"And he was interested in her?"

"Very much so. She had always been the image of him, and she seems to have grown up very nicely— something of a piano prodigy, I hear. He told me once that if anything happened to Sandra he meant to marry Lenore and take Edith over officially. Of course, that was all right with me."

"Then he'd given up the idea of a divorce?"

"Oh, yes. Sandra had grown too ill for anything like that, in the first place, and things had gone on too long the way they were to start changing. Francis is goodhearted, but he goes along as easily as he can."

"Do you think he meant it—about the marriage?"

"I'm positive about it. That's why this whole thing is so impossible. If Francis were the type of man to do such a brutal thing—which he's not—he'd have done it years ago, when Lenore might have been considered a kind of drag on him. But there's no possible motive, now. Sandra died last month, as I suppose you know, and he's absolutely free."

"In a way," Eggart admitted. "If you can call a man free who's so definitely committed."

"My dear fellow, if he hadn't wanted to marry Lenore, of his own free will, there was nothing to make him do it. Taking the ugliest possible view, if he and Lenore had reached a point where she tried to sue him I doubt whether she could even have got the case into court. Or what if she did, and even got some kind of settlement? Francis is well fixed financially; he could have stood it without any trouble."

"Is there any legal proof of Edith's paternity—any letters, for instance?"

Bellane looked at him levelly for a moment, and re-crossed his legs. "I don't know anything about letters," he said finally. "There is one document, in my possession, that I asked for at the time of our divorce. I didn't think it too much to ask, in the circumstances."

"When did you last see your brother, Mr. Bellane?"

"At Sandra's funeral. The twentieth of last month."

"How did he seem then?"

"Rather cut up. He was fond of her, too, oddly enough."

"Did he mention Mrs. Schafft or her daughter?"

"Well, no. Hardly."

"When did he tell you that he meant to marry Mrs. Schafft?"

"Oh, not so long ago. A year, or perhaps two."

"Had he told Mrs. Schafft the same thing?"

"Couldn't say. I expect so. I know he was seeing her—she was living in town, as you know." He gave an abrupt little sigh, and then stuck his pipe in his mouth and said through it, "Schafft, that's the name. I hadn't heard it before—all this. What sort of fellow is he?"

"He's a piano teacher—fifty-odd."

"I gathered that much. I meant, what sort of person?"

"Oh, quiet, reserved. He seems to have been good to the girl."

"Um," said Bellane, and looked as if he wanted to say more. "Does he know about this business about Lenore and Francis?"

Eggart grinned at him. "All I know is what you read in the newspapers, Mr. Bellane. Officially, that is. I'm sorry."

"It's all right. Shouldn't be asking, I suppose. Besides, I know you fellows don't overlook anything."

Eggart said they tried not to, and there was a brief, not very comfortable silence. Bellane crossed his legs again.

"Anything else I can tell you, Mr. Eggart?"

"You probably know that better than I do. If you can think of anything else, I'd be glad to hear it."

Bellane was quiet for a time, and then shook his head.

"That's the whole story, as I know it. I'm willing to swear that Francis and Lenore were on the best of terms, and that Francis told me he meant to marry her as soon as he could. You might get in touch with his lawyers—Weatherby, Weatherby & Long—and see if Francis mightn't have sent her there to see about getting free from this Schafft fellow. Perhaps not; it's a little soon, maybe, but you might try."

Eggart thanked him, and handed over the notebook in which he had been making a kind of précis of Bellane's replies to his questions. He was a little nervous about this, since the bare bones of the story, without the softening effect of question-and-answer and the general atmosphere of Bellane's pipe, made a bleak recital. Bellane frowned over it for some time, and Eggart made himself keep quiet. Fortunately, the last words were almost verbatim, and were evidently the point that Bellane was trying to make clear: that his brother was on good terms with Lenore, and had spoken voluntarily of marrying her. He nodded when he came to this, and held out his hand.

"I'll have to borrow your pen."

"Certainly."

"You might pass on my address to Francis. I'm not sure he remembers it. Tell him I'll be glad to come down if I can be of any use to him."

Eggart said he would, and put the notebook away carefully in his inner coat pocket. Bellane led the way back to the kitchen, where they found Mrs. Bellane and Emerson deep in a conversation that ended with their arrival. She looked at her husband with bright, measuring eyes, and said, "Coffee, dear?"

In the train once more, a few hours later, Eggart examined his impressions of the elder Bellane with some curiosity. They were mainly favorable, and he believed the story in his notebook to be true, and told without bias. What interested him was that he had got it so easily—merely by dropping one hint. He wondered if Bellane were really as open-minded as he thought himself, and whether he would have been equally frank if the story had been his own instead of his brother's.

It wasn't a point that needed to be decided. Cooney wasn't likely to inquire much beyond that signature. Paul Bellane as a suspect was out; he and his family had spent that Sunday night, soberly enough, at a church supper, and later with friends. The story was valuable only as a lever, to get the rest of the truth from Francis Bellane and the Schaffts, and he ought to be considering it as such.

So, reluctantly, Eggart closed the part of his mind that wanted to understand everything, relevant or not, and began sketching out a program for coming interviews.

Chapter Fifteen

On the day that Eggart arrived in Maine, Barney found himself saddled with a mission he would have been glad to pass on to almost anyone. And it was Theodore Schafft who had wished it on him.

The music teacher had come to Barney's door the night before, blinking curiously around the room as he talked, as if surprised to find this alien spot in the middle of his own domain. When Barney asked him to sit down he did so, carefully, as if the chair were someone else's and he were afraid of injuring it.

"I won't disturb you—I see you're studying. The fact is, I hoped you might be willing to do an errand for me—for us, that is. I've spoken to Mr. Bottman about it, and he's agreeable. In fact, he has added his own— Well, you see, this is all it is—to deliver this." He drew a sealed envelope from his pocket, and handed it over to Barney. It was addressed ready for mailing, to Miss Marja Bobrowicz, care of St. Vincent's Home, with the street and number.

"I had intended to mail it, at first, but it seemed a cold way to treat the poor child. And I should like someone to see her, and make sure that she is not unwell, or too distressed. Would you be willing to deliver the letter?"

It was a fairly heavy envelope. Barney took his shirt from the chair back, and tucked the letter in the pocket. "Money?"

"Not a great deal, of course. But her salary with us was not large, and it occurred to me she might not have been able to save anything to tide her over. Then, too, I thought a cordial note from her last employer might help her in finding another place."

He sighed, and lost Barney's place in *Moore* without noticing what he was doing. "I wouldn't mention it to Mrs. Schafft. Not that she would mind—but still, the whole thing is settled. No use to bring it up again."

Barney promised discretion, and asked how Edith was. She had remained at home, since the night they had all had dinner together, but had kept to her room. Bott was nearly back to normal, so Barney supposed he had made his peace somehow.

"She's fairly well. Of course, there's a period of readjustment—and for a sensitive mind, it mustn't be hurried." He closed Barney's textbook with great care, set it back on the table beside him, and got up. "You don't mind going? You needn't stay long."

Barney said he didn't, which was true at the time, but got less and less true as he thought about it. Marja in good spirits was one thing; but he began to have visions of her weeping and perhaps collapsing to the floor, in the middle of a large, bare room. Or a room full of other accusing orphans.

St. Vincent's itself reassured him a little. It was a large, matter-of-fact brick building in a crowded quarter of town, with a reception room that reminded him vaguely of the YMCA. He asked the first person he saw for Marja, was taken off to see one of the Sisters in charge, and presently left in another, smaller reception room until Marja could be produced.

She appeared with little delay, silent, but with shining eyes. The idea of a visitor to see her had struck her speechless with excitement, and Barney could get no answer to his attempts at conversation. Finally he handed over the envelope, and watched her examine it with great respect.

"Open it, Marja. It's for you."

She nodded, smiling, and turned it around a few times more. Then, with a quick gesture, she handed it back, indicating that he should open it for her. He tore the envelope and pulled out a folded sheet of paper, which opened to display a five and a ten dollar bill. Marja turned pale, and put her hands behind her back.

"It's yours, Marja. Fifteen dollars. Here."

All his attempts to get hold of one of her hands, and put the money into it, ended in defeat. He began to see that it was turning into a game, and suddenly put the money into his own shirt pocket. "Okay. If you don't want it, I'll keep it."

Marja laughed till the tears stood in her eyes, and a passing Sister put her head into the room and smiled sympathetically. After this the bills changed hands with no trouble at all, and he spread out the letter to read it to her. It was written in small, heavy script and said that the writer had found Marja Bobrowicz to be honest, hard-working and cheerful. The writer was, sincerely, Theodore Schafft.

"Meester Theo!" Marja said, round-eyed, and brought her finger down the center of the sheet. "He sends me this money?"

"He and Mr. Bottman."

Marja shook her head, and the smile faded. "Does the lady know?"

"Mrs. Schafft? I guess so. Anyway, it's your money."

"If I take it, she will make trouble for me, maybe."

"No, she won't. She's not angry at you, Marja."

"Oh, yes. She is angry."

"Well, whether she is or not, the money's yours," Barney said, and got up to go. "Give your letter to one of the nuns, Marja. She'll keep it for you until you get another job."

Without surprise, he discovered his shirttail in a viselike grip, and Marja still seated.

"I'm not a snooper, Meester Barney. But there are these things I hear, when I am working. That is not snoop."

Barney, who couldn't honestly agree, unclamped her brown fingers and said he wouldn't worry about it.

"I don't worry. It is she who worries, maybe. I don't think she sends me here because of what I say to this friend of yours, from the police. Oh, no. She thinks I have more to say after that, and there is no one here to listen."

"If you have any more to say, Marja, you ought to have said it to the lieutenant. Why didn't you tell him everything, when he was there?"

"I did, I did," Marja said instantly, and let go of him.

"You're sure?"

"Yes, I promise. I swear."

"Well, then, it's all right. Just forget about it."

Marja trailed him across the room, reassured enough to go on talking, but not very loudly.

"I don't forget, Meester Barney. I am trying and trying to remember. That lady is never afraid, and it makes her angry to be. She was angry with me, but not for what I said. If I could think what this is, that she has in her mind," said Marja candidly, "I would like to tell about it."

"I don't get it. She wasn't angry until you talked to the lieutenant, and she sent you away afterwards. That seems simple enough."

Marja wasn't listening. "There was the morning she locked her door. But I don't know why that was."

"Probably to keep you out."

"But I don't go in! I don't do that, when she is not up. If she is not up when I come downstairs, I only go into the kitchen and work there, and wait for her. I would never go into her room when she was in bed."

"Maybe she had her hair up in curlers."

"No, she was not even there. That is why I wondered. She had gone out very early to buy peaches for breakfast. I did not even know she was gone out until she came from her room and gave me those peaches. But she unlocked the door to come out! Now, that was very strange."

"How did she get into her room without you seeing her?"

"Oh, there is another door—through the room with Meester Theo's piano."

"Didn't she ever lock her room while she was out?"

"Never before, never!"

"How do you know?"

Marja looked at him angelically. "I go everywhere to clean, you see. And besides, these doors always stand open, from her room, when she is not in bed. There is one to the music room, and one to the dining room. Always open."

"Well, I don't know, Marja. Have you been in the room since?"

"But that day, even! And there was nothing!"

"You looked around, hey?" said Barney, grinning.

"I cleaned," said Marja with dignity. "Always on Mondays I clean."

"Monday? You mean it was last Monday she locked the door?"

Marja nodded, and looked pleased when he sat down again.

"Look, Marja—begin over, and let me get it straight. You came downstairs Monday morning, and her bedroom doors were closed. You thought she was still in bed. Right? What time was it?"

"Seven-thirty. Like always."

"Was she usually in her room when you came down?"

"Sometimes. Sometimes no."

"So you started to get breakfast. Then what?"

"Then I heard her turn the key of her door! I heard that very clearly, because I was in the dining room to fix the table, and I thought it was very funny she would unlock the door to let herself come out."

"And did she come out right away?"

"Oh, yes. With the peaches."

"Did she say anything?"

"No, she just gave me the peaches. But I think she was not pleased to have me be in the dining room, where I could hear that key turn. From the kitchen I would not hear it."

"Where would she get peaches that time of morning?"

Marja made a vague gesture. "There is a place. Not a store, but a place with no roof. In the winter it goes away."

"Had she ever gone out early like that before?"

"Oh, yes. Sometimes I went, and sometimes she went."

"Maybe she locked her door other times, and you just didn't hear it."

Marja said no, firmly, but added no reasons. Barney looked at her a minute longer, with a growing feeling of confusion, and then got up again.

"Then there's nothing unusual about the whole thing, except that she locked her door while she was gone?"

"She did lock the door," Marja repeated gravely.

"And you're sure it was last Monday?"

"Last Monday, yes. Was the lady dead then?" she asked suddenly. When Barney said yes, she was dead,

Marja looked disappointed. "Perhaps she was not quite dead? Perhaps that old lady took her away when she went to get the peaches?"

"No, no, Marja—that's impossible. You mustn't go around saying things like that, or you'll get in trouble."

Nevertheless he wondered, on his way across town, whether there had been something else that "the old lady took away, when she went to get the peaches." But what? And why lock the door, when she had got whatever it was out of the house?

The only reason he could see for locking up a room was to keep something inside from being discovered. But it was crazy to suppose that the something, whatever it was, would vanish while the old lady was out doing her shopping. Unless she had wanted to conceal the absence of something that had to be replaced? Not her own absence, certainly, since that was quite normal, but some object that she could get on her trip after the peaches?

He worried at this vague problem with increasing irritation until a sudden rush of business put it out of his head. Later in the afternoon it made an attempt to revive itself, turned out to make even less sense than during the morning, and was finally quashed. What if old Mrs. Schafft had locked up her room, for the first time in history? A growing suspicion of Marja herself might have been to blame; the old lady had made it clear that she didn't like "snoopers."

That night he reported to Schafft, who seemed relieved that Marja was bearing up under her disgrace. Bott gave their secret away a few minutes later by demanding to know, in a hearty voice, what kind of a place that asylum was, anyway? He had buttonholed Barney on his way upstairs, and Mrs. Schafft came into the hall behind him as he was speaking. Barney said, "Fine, fine"; and went on up, leaving silence behind him.

The next morning Mrs. Schafft bought peaches again.

Or something in a brown paper bag. She opened the screen door and stepped inside as he was coming downstairs, in the early morning quiet. The rest of the household was still in bed, as it always was when Barney left, and the entrance hall was dim, in spite of the front door standing open to let in the morning coolness.

She was wearing her usual neat housedress, with a light black coat over her shoulders and her plainly dressed hair uncovered, and she looked up at Barney and nodded quietly. He was seized with an instant and horrible feeling of guilt, as if all that he had heard and thought about her other peach-buying expedition were perfectly clear to her, and she had taken this means to reproach him.

He heard himself saying, in a jolly voice that seemed to bounce off the old walls, "You're out early this morning, Mrs. Schafft!"

"Yes, the goods are fresher."

He got his voice under control.

"Don't you even lock your door while you're gone? I mean the front door," he added insanely; and then, being only twenty, and painfully honest, turned bright red.

Mrs. Schafft regarded him calmly.

"No, this is a very quiet neighborhood." She stood still, to let him come up to her, and remarked: "So you went to see Marja yesterday?"

"Yes," he said, abandoning hope.

"My son has a good heart. This was a foolish gesture,

but if it did him good, there was no harm to it."

"I think it did everyone good, Mrs. Schafft."

"So you are sorry for Marja too? She told you how cruel I am, and you believe her?"

He couldn't match her smile, although it was a small one.

"Not at all."

"No, of course not. You're not so foolish as to listen to angry servant girls, Mr. Chance."

She nodded to him again, and went on into the living room. Barney told himself, out on the front porch, "That's enough. If I don't get out of here soon, I'll end up crazy or a policeman. Next rent-day I move."

Nevertheless it occurred to him later that moving was easier to think of than to do. There would have to be some excuse, and one that Bott would swallow. Offhand, he couldn't think of any.

He groaned, and wished for late September and the haven of the college dormitories. For the first time he thought he could appreciate what Lenore Bellane had been up against, in those quiet people in the old house in Brookline.

Chapter Sixteen

Cooney was pleased with the results of Eggart's trip, and spent a good part of the evening of his lieutenant's return in going over the new facts with him.

"I think we got a case," he said from time to time, with great gravity. "We can prove the kid is his, and that the mother had the screws on him. His wife's dead, and his alibi for not marrying the woman is gone. He has to choose between marrying her or losing the girl, and she gets him flustered by moving so fast, and he kills her."

"The main thing we've got to prove is how he came back."

"Oh, I don't know. I think Bellane's going to crack before we get through with him. His own brother's evidence, his own lawyer—I'm not giving up the tracing, you understand, but when you get a guy cold, with proof he's been lying his head off, you don't have to worry much longer."

"What about his own car?"

"He could have used it. The garage that services it for him says it didn't make any long trip—they keep the mileage checked, and the oil, and so on—but that's not foolproof. Personally, I think he got hold of some hedge-hopping pilot. If he did, I'll find out which one if I have to check every license in the country. I don't expect this to be easy, you know. The guy was deliberately laying a trail when he went home the first time. He had a long while to figure out another way of coming back."

There was a brief silence, and then Cooney added wistfully: "If we could just get hold of somebody that saw him around the hotel, that night! I don't understand how he done it!"

"It's not only the hotel, either. Whoever killed her had to get there, and get away. You'd think we'd get some results from such thorough checking."

"You been checking out Brookline way, too, huh?" said Cooney slyly.

"Sure. It doesn't hurt to be thorough."

"You're crazy for suspecting things," Cooney told him, not unkindly. "Somebody else has been out in Brookline, while you been gone, by the way."

"Bellane?"

"Yep. Every day. Ain't he a nice Uncle Francis,

though?"

"I wonder what the Schaffts think of that. And Bott."

"We ain't asked him. They let him in, that's all I know." He added, "I'd like to pull the phony bastard in tonight!"

"Let's get organized first," Eggart suggested. "I think we'll do better to spring this on him with a minimum of warning—just get him in for a quiet talk tomorrow, and then crack down. We'll have a better chance of seeing him go to pieces."

"I'll feel better when I get the key to his door," said Cooney.

"You have, more or less. He can't go anywhere." But Eggart was wrong. Bellane had escaped them before midnight, and the news reached the lieutenant just as he was getting into bed.

He was dressed in two minutes, and halfway downtown in five. The call had come through the local precinct station, whose men were already at the Standish when he arrived. Among the squad cars that blocked the curb, an ambulance waited, its doors wide.

Eggart was taken around back of the hotel where, on the grey concrete of the courtyard, the sprawled body of Francis Bellane was being painstakingly transferred to a stretcher. Two internes, grimly engaged, did not look up as he came to stand near them, as near as he could. Bellane's light silk dressing gown was crumpled, torn and stained; below it his trousered legs were awkward and unresisting; the cloth of one of them was badly ripped. It was only by the way they handled him that Eggart could tell he was not dead.

"When did it happen?" he asked the precinct officer beside him.

"Eleven-thirty, as near as we can get it. Several people heard him land, and looked out the window."

"You got the entrances blocked?"

The other looked startled. "No. You think ...?"

"Come on," said Eggart, and they left the silent group behind them and moved rapidly around the hotel.

By the time the ambulance with Francis Bellane in it had driven away, the hotel was sealed against the outer world. Nearly three-quarters of an hour had elapsed since the time of the fall—plenty of time for someone's exit; but Eggart, after a hurried check-up, doubted whether that exit could have been made unobserved. The hotel was small, and there was only one entrance open to guests. This had been under the eye of the night clerk and at least one bellhop, and the lobby—or "lounge"—was small enough so that anyone going out or coming in would almost certainly have been seen. The only other way out was through the back offices, intricate, and peopled with employees.

With this knowledge in his mind, Eggart felt the hard anxiety that had fastened around him begin to dissolve, and a subterranean excitement took its place. Something told him that his luck was in, this time. If anyone had pushed or thrown Bellane from his sixth-floor window, the chances were high that he was still in the hotel, waiting for a quieter time to leave.

"No one in or out till I get back," he left orders. "And I want a list of everyone that went through these doors tonight. Names if you've got 'em, and descriptions if you haven't."

Bellane was still alive when he got to the hospital, but still unconscious. That awkwardly crumpled leg had landed under him and been badly fractured; his shoulder was dislocated; they were still working on his skull, and believed the brainpan to be cracked, among other things. Eggart listened to the nurse with sinking hopes, but stubbornly.

"If he talks, I've got to see him. He's an important witness in a murder case. When can I see the doctor?"

The nurse couldn't tell him definitely, and he waited in antiseptic solitude until the young doctor came out to him. But even then there was nothing definite, except that they were doing the best they could.

"If we can get him through tonight, there's a chance. The trouble is, he was pretty much of a wreck before this happened. Not a chance in the world of your talking to him right away, I'm afraid."

Nevertheless Eggart waited, while the fight for Bellane's life went on. If they did lose him—if there were only a few seconds of lucidity at the end—he meant to be there.

Cooney surprised him by turning up, sleepy, and with Mahaney in tow, around two a.m. His calmness staggered Eggart, who had forgotten, in the night's turmoil, how far divergent their two viewpoints were.

"If we'd of pulled him in last night, this wouldn't of happened," Cooney reminded him, but without heat. "The guy must be a mind reader. Why can't they give him something to make him talk?"

The only thing that upset him was Eggart's precautions at the hotel. He heard about them with growing anger and surprise, and said, before Eggart had finished: "What are you trying to do—make it look like a double murder? The guy jumped, damn it! He was guilty, and he jumped! I want that guard taken off the doors pronto—you'll have every newspaper in town on our necks as soon as the guests try and get out in the morning!"

Eggart argued, but without success. They compromised finally on freedom for all bona fide guests, with quiet records to be kept of their comings and goings, and all strangers to be challenged, but gently. Neither was satisfied with the arrangement, but it stood; and Cooney himself went over to the hotel to see to it.

Mahaney remained with Eggart, and they wore an hour or so away together in gloomy silence. Empty beds were given them, to stretch out on, and Mahaney went promptly to sleep on his. Eggart, despite official promises that he would be called at any change in Bellane's condition, determined to stay awake. He thought he had, until a nurse wakened him, in broad daylight, to tell him that Bellane was dead.

He swung his legs off the bed instantly, hard eyes on hers.

"You didn't—"

"He never came out of it, Lieutenant. The whole thing was over in a couple of seconds. And you were so worn out, I hated to wake you afterwards. But if you'd like some good hot coffee, now ...?"

His watch told him it was seven, and the nurse, that Bellane had died a little after five. He swallowed his disappointment as best he could, and got up, shaking Mahaney.

"Okay, nurse; thanks. Sure. Coffee would be swell." It went down into his body like new blood, and brought a sudden idea in its wake.

"By God, what's the matter with me, Mahaney? I should have had a couple of men out in Brookline last night! The minute those hotel doors were unsealed, I should have— Come on; it's too late, but come on anyhow."

"Now, listen," the sergeant protested, hanging on to his half-empty cup. He discovered he was talking to air, and gulped the rest of the hot brew down as he got to his feet. It burnt his tongue, which hurt him all the way out to Brookline.

Waterford Street was sylvan at 7:30 in the morning, with mist still hanging in the early sunlight that slanted down between the old trees. But there was a fairly brisk traffic along the sidewalks; men with papers tucked under their arms, girls with fresh make-up and drugged eyes. A more solid and slowly moving figure caught Eggart's eye, and he drew in by 419 and laid a hand on Mahaney's arm.

"Wait a minute. Don't get out yet."

Mahaney's eyes followed the direction of the lieutenant's—back up the street the way they had come. The slow-moving figure was only a few houses away. He said:

"It's the old lady, ain't it?"

"Nobody else."

"Jeez, is that what—? You mean you knew she'd be—?"

"I didn't know anything. I still don't."

"What's she carrying?" Mahaney wondered, keeping his red neck twisted.

"We'll see. Come on."

They intercepted her at her own front walk, and she looked at them without surprise or pleasure. An unstylish dark coat hung open over her housedress, the early light lay gently on her pale hair, and her capable, ungloved hands were managing a black reticule and a brown paper bag. The top of this latter was open, and Eggart glanced in shamelessly.

"You do your shopping early, Mrs. Schafft."

"Yes. Are you coming here?"

"We are."

"My family is not up yet."

"I'm afraid you'll have to wake them. They're all here, I suppose?"

"Certainly. Why do you want them wakened?"

She paused at the screen door to free one hand, and Eggart reached out instead. The door opened easily on the entrance hall, left undefended in its mistress's absence; and Eggart, looking past her, saw Barney Chance coming quietly downstairs.

At the sight of the three of them—the old lady and her peaches, and the two red-eyed policemen with their beginning beards—the boy stopped short, and a peculiar expression slid over his face. Eggart, curious, watched him get under control and start down again.

"One of you is up, anyhow. 'Morning, Chance."

"What's the matter now?" said Barney, with an attempted grin.

"Francis Bellane's dead," said Eggart, to them both. "He died just a couple of hours ago."

The bag of peaches dropped suddenly to the floor, and its contents escaped in every direction. Eggart got a quick hand under Mrs. Schafft's arm, but she had no need of it. Only her head had gone down for a minute. She raised it, looked at him, and said dully: "Now it will begin all over again."

Then she started after the peaches. The three men forestalled her, and she stood in silence until a red-faced Mahaney put the bag back in her hands again.

"What happened to him?" Barney asked them, since she had not.

"Fell out a sixth-floor window," Eggart told him briefly, and turned away. "I'll go upstairs with you, Mrs. Schafft."

"Now?"

"Immediately, please."

Still in the black coat, and still carrying reticule and bundle, she began to mount the stairs with Eggart and Mahaney at her heels. Barney, his scalp pricking with excitement and dismay, watched them reach the landing and then vanish from his sight.

But not from his hearing. Overhead, Eggart said something brief to her and she replied even more briefly. Then there was a smart double knock on one of the doors, a pause, and another. From a difference in the sound, it seemed to be delivered on a different door. Schafft's and Bott's?

A part of Barney's mind knew quite well that this was not his affair, and that there was nothing to keep him standing there in the front hall with his attention straining upward. But another part of him was not in the least concerned with this knowledge. It had interests of its own, centering mainly around peaches.

The music parlor door stood open. He moved just inside it, and looked down the length of the room to where another door presented a closed surface. Behind this, he knew, was old Mrs. Schafft's bedroom.

Moving quickly and silently, Barney went toward that closed door and put his hand on the knob. It turned easily, but the door did not yield. Just to be sure, he put pressure on; it was firm as a rock. He dropped his hand and turned away. Locked. And then what?

Steps beginning the descent above him made him put on speed, and then come to a stop just inside the door. Whoever it was would see him from the landing if he came out of the music parlor. He remained just inside, leaning against the door frame as casually as he could, and waited. If she went through the living room portieres, across the hall, there was a good chance he would not be seen; but if she did catch sight of him, there must be nothing furtive about his attitude. He was just waiting there, near the front door, but out of the way.

She did, of course, sense his presence; he had known

that she would. But what he hadn't counted on was the effect of that slow, clear regard being turned full on him. Once more, she was responsible for his color changing—and changing drastically, he could tell from the feeling of it. Indignation at himself made him articulate.

"As long as Bott's getting up, I thought he might want me. I thought—I'd wait and see."

"In the music parlor?" she said, without smiling.

Above them began a confusion of masculine voices—kept low, for the most part, and speaking in fragmentary exchanges. Bott burst out in a few words—"Dead! My God, no! He—"; but someone checked him and he broke off, to resume in an inaudible mumble.

Mrs. Schafft went on looking at Barney.

"I don't think you'll be needed, Mr. Chance. I'd go on, if I were you."

She was right, he knew; but a forlorn clutch at dignity made him answer: "I'll wait a while on the front porch, and see," although there was nothing he wanted less to do.

They moved away from each other then, she into the living room and he out the screen door into the cool morning air. Here his color went down, and his embarrassment. By the time he had finished a cigarette he was near enough to normal to have gone off down the street on his own business without any more camouflage activity.

But by then he had had a chance to think his impressions over—and he went on waiting.

Chapter Seventeen

Bott either slept raw or had been interrupted in the process of dressing, to judge from the state in which he answered Eggart's summons. Schafft, on the other hand, delayed answering until he had pulled a cotton dressing gown over his faded pyjamas. But both of them were tousled and unshaven. If either was counterfeiting the appearance of a man just out of bed, Eggart could not have said which.

He told them his news briefly, said he wanted to talk to them as soon as possible, and left their incoherent questions unanswered as a guarantee of their speed in dressing. Bott, hanging onto his half-opened door, tried to get Eggart to come inside and "tell him about it, while he threw some clothes on." Eggart declined, and he and Mahaney went back downstairs to wait, and to seek out old Mrs. Schafft.

En route Mahaney remarked that they both looked like they'd been asleep, all right.

"In bed, anyway. That didn't prove anything, but it didn't hurt to try."

Penetrating through the closed blue portieres, and through the drawn-back, matching ones that marked the entrance to the dining room, they were drawn by faint sounds to the kitchen beyond and found Mrs. Schafft there, preparing coffee. She had taken off her coat and put away the reticule, and now looked just as always. The bag of peaches stood on the sinkboard, waiting attention.

She turned at their entrance, and put down the implement with which she was measuring coffee into the pot. Although her expression was under control and she said nothing much, Eggart was suddenly aware that she was shaken by inner emotion that she was trying to conceal.

"Did you tell them?"

"Yes. They're coming down. In the meantime, Mrs. Schafft, I'd like to know when Mr. Bellane was here last."

She turned away then, and resumed her occupation. "Yesterday. He was here every day, for three days, to see Edith. You must have known."

"You were willing to let him see her?"

"It was up to Edith. She was willing."

"Did any of the rest of you see or speak to him?"

"Of course. All of us. He had dinner with us last night."

"On good terms with you all?"

For a moment she did not answer; then: "If he was under suspicion, so were we all. It was better for Edith to see him with us than alone."

Heavy footsteps in the other room warned them of Bott's approach. He came in hurriedly, buttoning his shirt, and said to Mrs. Schafft, "I think Edith's up—I heard her moving around. She must have heard us—heard something ..." He spoke disconnectedly, his eyes going from Eggart to Mahaney, and one foot groping to pull out a kitchen chair. Mrs. Schafft poured boiling water over the coffee grounds and said:

"She will have to know, Edward. There is nothing I can do about that."

He had already forgotten her, and was staring hard at Eggart.

"Well, when did it happen? Did he leave a note? What made him do it?"

"You tell me," said Eggart, staring back. "You saw him yesterday, didn't you?"

"Yesterday, and the day before, and the day before that. I had a bellyful of him," Bott said, as if he were trying to produce something of his old brusqueness. But the mainspring was broken; he sounded dull and distracted. "Marthe, hasn't that coffee dripped yet?"

"What did he do out here so long? What did he talk about?"

Schafft appeared in the kitchen door, fully dressed, but somehow looking untidier than Bott in his shirtsleeves. Eggart turned to him.

"I suppose you talked to Bellane too, when he was here?"

"Yes, yes. We all did. He was not welcome, but he was a guest." He said to his mother, as if the others were so many shades, "Just as I was coming downstairs, mother, it came into my head—do you realize what this may mean to Edith? You remember what Bellane said yesterday, at dinner?"

Bott suddenly came to life.

"Don't make a fool of yourself, Theo. Saying and doing's two different things. He'd say anything to make a big noise!"

"What did he say?" Eggart demanded. They were all sitting around the kitchen table by now, and Mrs. Schafft was silently beginning to serve the fresh coffee. Mahaney watched her with bleared, hopeful eyes, and nursed his burnt tongue. She set a cup in front of him and he said, "Thank you, ma'am." Schafft turned to the lieutenant.

"Edith is his heiress, sir. Edith! He told us all at dinner, only last night. In those very words. 'Edith is going to be my heiress,' he said. 'She is the closest relative I have next to my brother, and the dearest person in the world to me.' He was quite serious—how serious, I didn't realize at the time. Poor fellow, poor fellow!"

"That right, Bott?"

Bott's eyes had hardened again. "That's what he said."

"But you don't think he meant it?"

"If he meant it," said Bott, "he made himself a will before he jumped. Did he?"

"Why then? Did he say he was going to make such a will, or already had?"

"He already had, as I understood him," Schafft said, drawing together his heavy brows in thought. "The way he said it—'Edith is going to be my heiress'– sounded as if he had already made his arrangements. I got that impression at the time, very strongly. Perhaps there was something else said—I don't remember exactly."

Bott gave a short laugh, and held out his cup to be refilled. "Don't count that money till you see it, my friend. He hadn't made any will. He hadn't even thought of it ten minutes before he said that. He was just feeling sentimental, and wanted to make a splash. There's no will, unless it's down there in his hotel room. Is it?"

"We haven't finished examining his things." Bott looked at him a minute longer, and then went back to his coffee.

"I'm right. You'll see I'm right. There's no will."

"I agree with you, Edward," Mrs. Schafft said unexpectedly. "I believe Mr. Bellane spoke on impulse."

"Why?"

"It is only an impression. No doubt the lieutenant knows better than we which of us is right."

Schafft, thus reminded, turned to Eggart with queries about Bellane's death. Eggart told them as much as he wanted them to know, and they listened in silence, with their eyes fixed on their cups or the

table before them. This second death seemed to have
affected them more than the first, for some reason.
Or two of them, Eggart corrected himself. Schafft,
while grave and shocked, showed no signs of breaking
down or leaving the room as he had done during their
first interview. It was he, in fact, who answered most
of the lieutenant's questions as to what Bellane had
said or done during his visits. To get a direct reply
from Bott or old Mrs. Schafft, he found that he had to
address them directly. But the information he got from
all three was much the same. Bellane had been diffi-
dent, polite, and persistent. He had not tried to hold
conversations with any of them but Edith, but had
been pleasant when one of the others was in the room.
He had said almost nothing about himself and little
about Lenore, except for conventional expressions, but
he was willing to talk and to hear about Edith indefi-
nitely. Apparently it was on this precarious footing
that the unwelcome visitor had spent his three days
in the Schafft household. His attempts to take Edith
out with him old Mrs. Schafft had quashed, but he
had taken this in good part, and showed up the next
day with more little gifts and the same amiable manner. Nobody had liked him, except Edith.

It was Eggart who told her of his death, and curiously enough, the others let him do so. She came into
the kitchen while they were seated around the table
and stood in the doorway, her dark hair down her
back and her eyes apprehensive in a white face. She
said, "What's wrong?" to all of them, and Eggart told
her. Only Schafft watched her receive the news, and
got up to place her chair in silent sympathy; Bott sat
with his eyes fixed on his cup, and old Mrs. Schafft
was making another pot of coffee.

The girl took it very quietly. She sat down, with her

hands in her lap, and just stared—from one to the other of them.

"Dead? But he was just here—it was only last night ..." Some fatal repetition in the phrase seemed to light, in her mind, the connection between the two deaths. She said bleakly, "How?" and Eggart told her that too, as gently as he could.

Bott, as if inaction were becoming unbearable, got up himself and went after coffee for her; but he still did not speak. Eggart let her turn it over in her mind in silence. Finally she lifted her eyes once more—heartbreaking under their strong brows—and looked directly at him.

"I know what you think," she told him, with lips that scarcely moved—and then dropped her head on the table and began to cry as if her heart would break.

Embarrassment and restlessness seized the rest of them. Mahaney growled in his throat; Schafft leaned over to comfort her with shaking hands; Bott, at the cupboard, broke two saucers without saying a word; and old Mrs. Schafft gave up her coffee-making and turned to watch, with set lips.

"What do *you* think?" Eggart asked her, when she brought her sobbing under control. Her head, still resting against the table and with its disordered hair around it, moved listlessly.

"I don't know—I don't know. Last night he was talking about his will. Why should he have done that, unless ...? But he seemed so cheerful—so much like he always was ..."

A peculiar croaking sound startled them all. It was Bott, who had stuck grimly to his purpose and was now trying to bring a cup of steaming coffee to Edith's attention. Always obedient, she sat up to take it as soon as she discovered what was required of her; but she set it down at once on the table and turned back to Eggart.

"No! I shouldn't have said that! He didn't mean to die—any more than mother did. You don't believe he meant to, do you?"

"It's too soon to be sure," Eggart replied; but she was no longer listening to him. The full horror of Bellane's implied suicide appeared just then to strike her—and the motive he might have had. She gave a little moan, openmouthed, as if something inside were hurting unbearably, and then shut her lips and was silent.

Eggart smothered an impulse to get up and leave by embarking on a new series of questions to the others. He would like, he told them, every detail of Bellane's visits; everything they could remember him saying; whether his attitude had been the same on all three days and if not how it had changed. A kind of nervous volubility seized Schafft and Bott—due, Eggart suspected, to Edith's silent presence. Even old Mrs. Schafft joined them at the table and put in a word from time to time. They did their best, remembering the most trivial exchanges, the almost exact times of Bellane's comings and goings; his few cautious words about Lenore were dragged out at great length, with each correcting the other as to precise phrasing.

Eggart was patiently attentive—to what they said, to how they said it, and to every gesture that was made. Mahaney's eyes became glazed; he turned into a pathetic machine for acquiring and disposing of hot coffee, and it did him no good whatsoever.

Nearly half an hour of his martyrdom went by before Eggart turned back to Edith. Her skin had gained a little color, and the old lady, perhaps to distract her, had gone around the table to begin the elaborate hair-braiding which must have been a morning ritual.

Edith sat passive under it, and turned as passively to receive Eggart's questions.

Yes, she and her uncle had had many long "talks"—some of them about himself, about his loneliness, and how close he felt to her. He had wanted to know all about her training, her plans, and what she wanted to do and be. She had told him everything he wanted to know. "I felt sorry for him, somehow. He did seem lonely."

"Did he suggest your going to New York with him?" Eggart asked. The others were silent, and Edith looked at him in surprise, and not happily.

"He—yes, he asked me if I would like to. He wanted to arrange for me to study with Maxim Gubaryov—he said it was possible."

"And what did you say?"

"I told him that Uncle Theo made my plans," said the girl dully. The last braid went around her neat head, and old Mrs. Schafft drew a pin from her pocket to fasten it in place. None of them spoke. Eggart turned to Schafft.

"Did Bellane speak to you about this?"

"No."

"Would you have approved?"

"What's the use of discussing it? It's not a thing to be decided in a minute. And now that Bellane's dead, the question's closed. We couldn't possibly afford it."

"Maybe Edith can," said Bott, expressionless. Edith told him passionately, "I won't have you all getting your hopes up—"

"My hopes!" Bott exclaimed. "What do I want with his damned money? Who needs it? You never told *me* about this Gooby—this Goober—this fellow in New York! My money's as good as Bellane's, isn't it?"

"Please, please!" Schafft interrupted, and pushed

them back into silence with one imploring gesture. Eggart, whose head felt empty and humming with fatigue, got to his feet. Mahaney blinked, and scrambled up beside him.

"I won't keep you any longer now. You may have to come down to headquarters later in the day—please don't get out of touch with the house, here, until you hear from us."

"We'll be here," said Bott grimly. Schafft got up to take the two police officers to the door.

On the front porch Eggart paused a minute, blinking his tired eyes against the now strong morning sunlight. A thin figure got up from the porch railing and approached him. He turned his head and saw the dark, serious face of Bott's driver, looking very young and a little nervous.

"Is Bott going downtown, do you know?"

"I don't think so. Why?"

Barney hesitated, and then his shoulders moved, under their thin shirt, in a shrug. "No reason, I guess. You couldn't give me a lift down, could you?"

"Sure. Come on."

Mahaney was already stretching his legs in the back seat; Eggart always drove. Barney got in at his side, in a kind of explosive silence that reached the lieutenant's attention, tired as he was.

"What's with you, fella?" he asked; and Barney turned sideways to face him, his young mouth set.

"Just tell me one thing, Lieutenant—did Bellane jump, or was he pushed?"

"You tell me."

"You mean there's nothing to show, one way or another?"

"Supposing there was?" Eggart glanced at him, and then glanced again. "What is it? What have you got hold of now?" When Barney did not reply at once, he added, without his official briskness: "Come on, let's have it, Barney. You've got a good level head on you, and anything that worries you worries me too. I want to know what it is."

"Who's worried?" said Barney, turning red with pleasure.

"You are. You've noticed something, or somebody's told you something, and you don't know what to make of it. Which?"

"Both. I'm tempted to tell you just because it's so darned crazy, but if Bellane jumped himself out that window there's no reason to drag it out—"

"Well, between us, I don't think he did," said Eggart calmly. There was a strangled sound from the back seat, and Eggart added without turning: "Between the three of us, I mean. This whole thing is off the record, so get it off your chest, Barney. What's crazy?"

"Well, you noticed the front door when you got there this morning, didn't you? The way it was wide open, and you just had to pull open the screen door and walk in?"

"Yeah."

"She says that's because it's a quiet neighborhood— old Mrs. Schafft, I mean. Okay, I guess it is. But then why does she lock up her bedroom when she goes? And Marja says it never happened before Edith's mother died. That was the first time—that Monday. And this morning it happened again."

Chapter Eighteen

The expectancy had drained out of Eggart's face— Barney saw it go—but he repeated politely: "Locked her bedroom? You mean upstairs?"

"No, she sleeps downstairs. I told you this was nuts, but here's the way it goes. You know Marja's gone back to St. Vincent's? Well, Schafft got to worrying about her, and he and Bott put up some money for her and sent me over to deliver it. Marja was fairly cheerful, and so on, but she couldn't seem to figure out why old Mrs. Schafft had sent her away. She was convinced it wasn't over what she told you about the divorce—I don't know why; this is all from Marja's viewpoint—and that the old lady was afraid she had something else to spill. The trouble was, Marja didn't know what, herself.

"She said the only thing out-of-the-way that she had noticed was on last Monday, when she came down to get breakfast. There was no sign of Mrs. Schafft, and her bedroom door was closed. That did happen some-times, apparently, so Marja went ahead getting break-fast. The rest of them were upstairs sleeping, as usual. Well, she happened to be in the dining room fixing the table when she heard the key turn in Mrs. Schafft's door, and out she came with a bag of peaches. She said she had been out early to get them, and Marja admits that's nothing unusual. What got her curiosity up was the old lady coming through her bedroom that way, and unlocking the door to get out. She says it's never been locked before, and that Mrs. Schafft didn't seem very pleased about her being in the dining room at the time and noticing it."

"Maybe she was starting to get suspicious of Marja," Eggart suggested.

"That's what I thought too, but I didn't like to say so. But then why should she lock her room up again this morning, now that Marja's gone? And leave the rest of the house open?"

"How do you know she did?"

"I went and tried the door."

Eggart chuckled. "You're no engineer, Barney. Give it up, and I'll get you on the force."

"If I lose my fellowship, I'll take you up," said Barney with gloom. "If I'm starving to death at the same time, that is. Aren't you glad I told you?"

"It's interesting," Eggart reassured him. "Offhand I can't think of any answer. Is there a back stairs?"

"I don't think so, no."

"How are the rooms laid out downstairs? Where is her room?"

"Back of the music parlor, where Schafft gives his lessons. That's the room to the left of the front door, as you go in. There's one door to her room on the music parlor, and one on the dining room. Marja says they're always left open, so people can make short cuts, I guess."

"So she isn't fussy about people going through her room. Well. I don't know, Barney—what reason could she have? What could she be keeping in there?"

"Nothing. Marja says she gave the room a good cleaning later in the day, last Monday. It was open anyway, and she didn't find a thing."

"How soon after she came back did she open up the room?"

"Right away, I guess. She did this morning, anyway. I got tired of waiting there on the porch and came in to see if I could find Bott. I heard you all out in the kitchen and came as far as the dining room archway, and I could see her door standing open. That made me curious enough to go back and try the other door— the one into the music room. Or I didn't have to try it—I could see that it was wide open, too."

Eggart's eyebrows went up, but he made no comment. A sudden and convulsive snore from the back seat expressed Mahaney's opinion; Barney noted it with depression. He hadn't been particularly anxious to meddle for a third time in the Schaffts' affairs, mainly because he himself could make nothing of the scrap of information that had come his way. It was this very uncertainty that had pushed him to confiding in Eggart—that, and the shock of the morning's news—and now he could see what a scrap it was, devoid of his own imaginings.

He made no attempt to excuse himself, however, and sat mute until Eggart spoke again.

"What's this shopping-before-breakfast deal? Is it something new?"

"Marja says not. Sometimes the old lady went, and sometimes she sent Marja—there's a kind of open-air market that opens early."

"The old lady is always up before the family?"

"That's the way I understand it. I know I never meet any of them on my way out, around seven-thirty, except her."

"What about the nighttime? Do they all go to bed together? At the same time, I mean?"

"I think so."

"It's a funny setup," said Eggart vaguely. "The whole house, that is. A little hard on the girl, I should think."

Barney detected an easy letdown in this switch to the general, and responded accordingly. Conversation died out, and nothing was heard but Mahaney's intermittent choking until Eggart slowed up to let Barney out at his corner. But his voice was friendly as he remarked: "I think I'd keep the door situation under my hat for a while. Just for policy."

Barney said "Sure," thanked him for the ride, and walked off very briskly in the morning sunshine. Mahaney, wakened by their stop, looked after him and shook his head.

"These college kids. The ideas they don't get in their heads."

"That's the penalty for a mind that works overtime," Eggart replied, and let his sergeant consider this during the rest of the ride.

Back at headquarters, Eggart found Cooney waiting for him, keyed-up and impatient but in good spirits.

"We want to get going while this is still hot," he said at once. "Where have you been? I want to get over to the hotel and pick up his stuff, too. It doesn't look like he left anything, but we got to make sure."

"There's some talk about his having left a will in favor of the girl. I'd like to get on the trail of that right away—check his own lawyers, and the local ones. It's probable he made it in the last few days, if he made it at all—and he may not have."

Cooney, hearing that the information came directly from the Schaffts, as did his lieutenant, was doubtful.

"What do you want to go rushing out there for? We got to move carefully till we get this thing fixed up, Eggart. We can't come out and *say* he killed her and then jumped when we began to close in on him—but unless we make boobs of ourselves, we don't have to. The newspapers'll say it for us, clear enough. Or maybe you don't think that's the way it was?"

Eggart, aware of sudden sharpness in Cooney's voice, replied that there didn't seem much proof one way or the other, yet.

"Proof! What do you want? What about his own story? She got him up here for one thing—to help her ask for a divorce. Did he? No—he turned and cut it out of here as quick as he could, as soon as he found out what she was up to. That stuff about her not telling him anything is eyewash. She told him all right, and he wasn't having any part of it. So does it make sense to think he'd just high-tail it out of here and let her go ahead and try for that divorce he didn't want? Not on your life. He stopped her as fast as he could—and we stopped him!"

"Do you want to wait before we look into the will?"

"I do not. Everything we find out will make it that much surer. There's only one reason for making wills in a hurry, and I wouldn't be surprised if he did."

Cooney was right, as they learned not many hours later. It was not necessary to check with any Boston law firm; their first inquiry brought the information they sought. Bellane had made a recent will, and with his own lawyers. But not within the last week. It had been made immediately following his wife's death, and a Mr. Weatherby was on the point of leaving for Boston to give his client a last, melancholy representation—and, he was willing to admit, to contact the Schaffts. Which meant that undoubtedly Edith came in for a good part of Bellane's estate, if not most of it, Eggart surmised. He hung up without intimating where Mr. Weatherby would have to go to contact his client now—which was the morgue—and passed on the information to a gratified Cooney.

"Precautions. You see? She was pushing him hard even then."

For a hard-pushed man, Bellane had packed with remarkable care and attention—or else some member of a well-trained household staff had done it for him. Cooney, who was present at the examination of Bellane's effects, came close to enjoying himself.

"Look at this," he said, reverently unfolding a tie. "Twenty bucks if it's a nickel—want to bet?"

"How would I know, on my salary?"

"And look at these shirttails! Jeez, he could have tucked them in his shoes. And look at that collar— that's no laundry job. Or if it is, I'd like to find out what laundry."

With one thing and another, by the end of a long afternoon Eggart found himself in a state of suppressed exasperation that was near the breaking-out point. It wasn't Cooney, exactly, or young Mr. Weatherby, or even Mahaney who was to blame. At least, he didn't think so. He felt a little like a man who has looked up the answer to an involved mathematical calculation, and still doesn't understand how it is arrived at. There was the problem, and there was the answer; and the steps in between were depressingly obscure.

He went out to dinner a little early, and pampered himself by making a longer than usual trip to a famous chophouse, where he chose his dinner with care and sat a long time over it. That business about the old lady's doors had begun to worry him again, just as part of the general perversity of things. That she should lock up her own room so carefully and leave the rest of the house wide open argued that her precautions were not against the world at random but against her own family—or some member of that family—in particular. But which one? And why? If she distrusted one of them, it would be Bott sooner than her son or the girl; but if she suspected him of searching her things in her absence, it would be simpler to give up the peaches than to go through such a rigamarole.

A door was locked for one of two reasons: protection, or concealment. Protection meant nothing to him so far; concealment had to be of *something*—or even the absence of something. Herself? But her own morning absence was a regular affair. Perhaps that was why?

Perhaps someone could count on her being gone from a silent house at least one morning in the week? He found himself going in circles here, with unexplainable visions of Bott coming back to mind, and ordered another beer with his dinner. Then he had beer to follow, and sat on feeling his taut mind relax.

Presently a curious idea occurred to him—and on the heels of it, a method by which he might test it immediately. He began going through his pockets eagerly, examining in his hand the miscellany he brought up from each (he was a bachelor) with surprise and contempt before putting them back. Finally he found what he was after: two shabby and much creased folds of paper. These he smoothed open on the table before him.

Schafft had brought them to Eggart from his mother's hand, not many days before; one was the name and address of Francis Bellane's legal firm, and the other bore the name "Mrs. Mabel Bottman" and a street address in South Boston. He looked at these with approving eyes, and then tucked them carefully away in his wallet.

Then he got his hat and went to pay his bill, a much more cheerful man than he had come in.

Chapter Nineteen

The evenings when Barney had really enjoyed coming home from work, had walked with pleasure up the old, tree-lined street and come with relief into the dim quietness of his room, had already begun to seem as far back as prehistoric times. Since his first interview with Eggart, he had walked up those porch steps with increasing reluctance, and finally with actual distaste. If it wasn't so near the end of the summer that a change seemed insane ... if it wasn't for the difficulty of explaining to Bott, and the others ... if only he had left at the beginning of the affair, when his going might have seemed to come more from courtesy than panic ...

All these things went around in his mind as he came within sight of the Schafft house every evening; but now, tonight, he knew he had reached rock bottom. That confidence to Eggart in the police car seemed to him now not only inexcusable, but the action of a madman. And a malicious madman, to boot. Every step he took inside these people's house was an insult to their trust and hospitality. He almost longed to be discovered, and thrown out on the street with appropriate curses.

Or, if that were impossible, at least he hoped to get up to his room without meeting any of them face to face and having to bear their kindly greetings. In this he was successful, although the blue portieres, for the first time in memory, were pushed back to give a view of the empty living room and to let out the sounds of the family dining in the room beyond. This unveiling of the Schafft privacy was probably caused by the heat, which had been gradually renewing itself all week and now hung over them in even greater force than on the preceding weekend. But it did just flash through Barney's burdened mind that he, and not the heat, might be responsible. If anyone were waiting for him to come home—were waiting to confront him with his villainy—they had ample notice of his arrival. You couldn't get up those uncarpeted stairs without making some kind of noise.

However, nobody paid any attention to him. He got unchallenged to his room, peeled down as usual, and went in for his usual shower. By the time he settled down to study, he was beginning to feel almost safe. To his surprise, there was even a little subdued piano music, played, he thought, by Edith. He didn't know what the music was, but it sounded rather sad, and went on for nearly half an hour. Gradually he found himself listening instead of reading, and when the last notes trailed away his disturbances had gone with them and left him feeling soothed and a little drowsy.

He shut his book, yawned, and got up to cross to the wide, inviting bed that waited for him, when suddenly it happened. Someone whose knock at the door he didn't recognize wanted to speak to him.

He redressed hastily to a condition of decency and went to answer. Mrs. Schafft was outside, with a dish of some pale yellow concoction in her hand. It was apparently not for him, though, since she made no reference to it and only asked if she might come in. He was nervously cordial, got a grip on himself, and discovered that the alternative was an equally nervous silence. Mrs. Schafft was exactly as usual. She sat in his easy chair, put down her dish, and glanced calmly about the room. His discarded socks were defenseless in front of her, but she did not appear to notice them.

"Where did you go this morning? Mr. Bottman inquired for you."

"Oh—did he? I understood he wasn't going down—"

"From whom? The men from the police?"

"Lieutenant Eggart, yes. I was waiting on the porch, and he came out and said he thought Bott was staying."

"Then you must have had a very long wait, all for nothing," she observed, almost kindly. Barney murmured something, and she went on: "I thought at one time you were coming in to join us, and have coffee.

You should have."

"I didn't like to interrupt you."

"You still look at us through Marja's eyes, I'm afraid."

"Oh, no. That is, Marja hasn't any—any feeling—"

"Hasn't she?" she interrupted in her quiet voice. "I'm afraid she has, Mr. Chance. And not a very pretty feeling. There's no need to tell you what."

There was a need, but he felt shy of expressing it. Perhaps she had expected him to, for she waited a moment before continuing: "That was my real reason for sending her away. She had got a very unpleasant idea in her mind, and it seemed too much to put up with Marja's ideas on top of everything else."

A vague wonder that he could ever have thought her taciturn slid through Barney's mind. She could speak, when she chose, very easily and well, and with neither the embarrassment nor the 9ververbosity of the habitually silent. He made himself say:

"An unpleasant idea?"

"As you know."

Francis Bellane could have handled this situation very well, or Eggart. There were a great many ways of sending the ball back to her: "I don't think I do," or even vague murmurings or a flat "No, I don't know." But he did know; and caught off-balance as he was could not pretend otherwise. She watched his embarrassed silence with a little smile, and added: "I think you owe it to me to tell me just what is responsible for Marja's attitude."

"I don't think she has an attitude, Mrs. Schafft."

"Nonsense, Mr. Chance. Don't make mysteries out of a foolish servant girl. We have enough to worry us without that."

This was a reasonable speech, but Barney's own reaction to it was not. Whether it was the contempt it showed for poor Marja, or the concealed contempt which she had, he was sure, for himself, and all other outsiders, Barney's resistance stiffened. He said almost sullenly, "Then Marja's the person you ought to talk to, Mrs. Schafft."

She was not offended, although she waited before answering.

"I suspect you're as much of a child as she, Mr. Chance. I can see she's infected you with some bogey, and you're determined to guard it."

This time he did manage to sidestep. "I don't understand what you mean by bogey."

And then suddenly he saw that she was angry. Whether she had been so before and betrayed her feeling now by some slight change of expression, some involuntary movement, or whether anger had leaped alive in her at his reply, he could not tell. But he was sure it was there even before she spoke.

"You're ridiculous children, both of you. Do you suppose that because I'm an old woman, I'm blind? You're behaving exactly as Marja did before she went away— you don't look me in the face—you positively blush when you speak to me, and it's all since you went to see that girl. I tell you, I want to know what this nonsense is about! I expect you to tell me!"

"I haven't any nonsense to tell you, Mrs. Schafft," he said doggedly.

She was silent, and did not look at him; he had an impression she was ashamed of having lost her temper, and meant to get it under control. Or else she regretted having been so frank, and for so little. Finally she looked up—not at him, but past him—and sighed.

"Well. Perhaps I've misjudged. It's easy for the old and the young to misunderstand one another, and you're very young—and I'm rather old."

He wanted to put an end to it, somehow, anyhow, but right then.

"I'm sorry. I'm not a very satisfactory roomer, I know."

"At least you will be willing to tell me that Marja has made you no confidences? To give me your word?"

"What sort of confidences?" he stammered.

She didn't explain, but let her eyes come to meet his with such an intent, curious expression that his embarrassment died at once and a kind of cool despair took its place. She wasn't listening to what he said, he felt that she didn't even care; it was as if her question had been put for some answer other than speech, and as if she had taken that answer from him by her look. He said nothing else, and she did not seem to expect him to.

She got up, and smoothed down her housedress with a gesture he had often seen her make, and began to walk slowly toward the door.

"Don't let us quarrel. We're all of us upset. We must make allowances, I suppose. Please make them for me, at any rate."

"You've forgotten your pudding," he said miserably, picking it up, and she turned at the door to regard the proffered dish without interest.

"It's all right. I brought it for you."

Coals of fire, certainly. "That's very nice of you, but I've had dinner—"

"Keep it; eat it. To show there are no 'hard feelings,' as you would say."

She gave him a little, tired smile and opened his door before he could do it for her. A rush of honesty made him articulate at last.

"I'm the one who ought to apologize, Mrs. Schafft. In the first place I should never have stayed on here at a time when you and your family ought to have been alone, and then—"

She held up her hand in a quick, imperative gesture for silence, and stepped out into the hall. He put the dish down and followed her, alarmed, and then stopped as he saw there was no one there.

The voices came from downstairs, from the front door. Schafft's deep one was rumbling, "I think so, gentlemen; I think so. Please come in." And Eggart's was audible, as he evidently accepted the invitation. "This is Mr. Bircher, Mr. Schafft. If we may just have a few words ..."

The rest was drowned in the rustle of Mrs. Schafft's dress as she crossed the hall, and in the quick sound of her footsteps. At the top of the stairs she paused again, as if to listen; she had forgotten Barney completely. But only the vaguest of sounds drifted up now; Schafft had apparently taken the men into the living room.

Mrs. Schafft hesitated only a minute, and then began to descend the stairs. Barney went on standing there, outside his open door, with an instinctive readiness to help which her urgent manner had left with him. But there was no need of his help. He heard her cross the lower hall with the same firm tread, heard the stir of masculine voices that her coming aroused, and then a settling back into quietness again. If they were speaking at all now, in the living room, it was in such low voices that no echo of it came upstairs. To stand there any longer would simply be an exercise of curiosity—the kind that had already gotten him in over his head.

Nevertheless he moved back into his own room with reluctance. What was Eggart doing here, again? And who was Mr. Bircher? Some new police official? Did that mean something new had come up?

He gave his door a halfhearted push that did not quite close it, and let it stay that way. Then he wandered over to his chair—the one Mrs. Schafft had recently left—and sat down in it. Nearby stood Mrs. Schafft's peace offering—a kind of floating island, he thought, examining it with idle curiosity. It looked untidy, but good. All Mrs. Schafft's food that he had come in contact with was good.

But she had forgotten to give him a spoon. He registered this fact without any particular feeling, and went on sitting there. He felt as if he were waiting for something. Perhaps it was only to quiet down, to think over what had been said here in the room a few minutes ago. He made an attempt to go over their conversation, but without success. The silence around him was too oppressive.

A sudden resurgence of voices from downstairs brought him relief. He listened unashamedly, but could hear nothing definite. They were too far away, and the house was too well-built; he couldn't distinguish one word. Yet, from the confusion and dim harshness of those muffled voices, he could tell that this was not merely a conversational exchange. His heart skipped lightly, once, as he thought: They're quarrelling.

He got up and walked quietly to his door. Just as he reached it, some kind of faraway concussion sent its abrupt echo up through his floor. What? Something in the back of the house—under his room? He came out into the hall, cat-footed, and paused. It came again, and then again—heavy thumps. Fighting? Were they fighting?

Edith's door pulled open, and her startled face peered out and turned to his.

"Barney—what is it?"

"I don't know. Stay here, Edith—I'll find out."

He went down three steps at a time, no longer trying to be unheard, because the noise from below was greater than any he made. He ducked into the empty living room, raced through it and the equally empty dining room, and came to a kitchen unexpectedly full of people. Bott and Schafft were there, and Eggart and Mahaney, and the unknown Mr. Bircher, slight and deadly pale, half behind the icebox. The rest of them were crowded against the closed cellar door, and Mahaney, Eggart and Bott were alternately throwing the weight of their heavy shoulders against it, or heaving in unison. There was a confused roar of male voices, over which Eggart's abruptly rose, commanding.

"Wait a minute—get back, all of you. Mahaney, try a couple of shots at the lock."

"My God, you can't do that!" Schafft's voice was agonized. "You'll hit her!"

Mahaney, red-faced and deaf to any voice but Eggart's, already had his .45 out of its holster and was releasing the safety; Schafft caught at his arm and was pulled back by Bott, and then the whole confusion of sound and movement was blotted out by one tremendous blast. It silenced every one of them; they stood there like terriers at a rathole, their faces strained, listening for some sound which did not come. Mahaney lifted his arm and the .45 spoke again, splintering another hole in the wooden door.

Eggart said at once, "Okay—hold it!" and worked momentarily at the hardware with his fingers. In a moment he pulled the door back, displacing the tense figures behind him, and the dark entrance yawned before them. Without a word he dropped downward, three steps at a time, with Mahaney after him.

Bott, muttering, was on their heels; Schafft followed

him more slowly, one hand outstretched and shaking perceptibly. In the kitchen there were left only Barney and the stranger, who seemed on the point of collapsing.

"What's the matter?" Barney asked him.

The man leaned against the icebox, tried to speak, and finally croaked: "I don't know—she said she had something cooking—we waited, and she didn't come back ..."

A sudden shifting of his terrified eyes warned Barney, and he turned to find Edith in the doorway. He moved toward her at once, to keep her from coming any farther.

"Edith, if you'd just—wait ..."

The stranger was babbling on; once started he did not seem to be able to stop. "It's my fault—I shouldn't have come. They shouldn't have brought me! She just looked at me once. 'I've got something in the oven,' she says—"

A loud, hoarse cry from under their feet struck him dumb, and made Barney's skin come up in points. In itself the cry was a lost, agonizing sound; magnified by the cellar's stones it lost all human quality. The strange little man began to whimper incoherently, and Edith darted under Barney's outstretched arm and made for the open entrance to the cellar. Just as he caught up to her they were both blocked by a large form hastily mounting the stairs below them. It was Mahaney.

He glared briefly at Edith, and then at Barney.

"Get her away from here," he growled, and brushed by them without a glance for the little man behind the icebox, who gibbered at him, and then fell into silence. He had seen, as they all did, the sergeant's blood-soaked cuffs and sleeves, and the red streaks on his hands. None of them said another word, but Barney felt Edith's whole weight fall against him.

He caught her as best he could, threatened the stranger into helping him, and so presently got her into the living room, on the couch. Mahaney's voice, explosive with haste, burst down on them from the telephone on the landing.

"I don't care what you send, but send it now! We're getting tourniquets on her, but that ain't half enough. Send an ice wagon if you have to, but get it here pronto!"

He slammed down the receiver and tramped down the stairs and through the portieres. Barney left Edith's side and came up to him.

"The old lady?"

"Yeah." He kept going.

"She's not dead?"

"She ain't far from it."

Barney waited until they reached the kitchen door and then asked, "Suicide?"

"Naw, her wrists busted open," said Mahaney violently, and ducked his head to enter the cellar stairway.

Barney let him go, feeling nausea rise up in him in one strong wave. The wave went down, and he turned to the kitchen sink, filled a glass with cold water, and took it slowly back into the living room.

Chapter Twenty

It was night in the hospital, night in the long corridors with their impersonal and uniform lighting, night in the shadowy rooms glimpsed now and then through half-open doors. On the composition floor even

Cooney's heavy tread was absorbed into the nocturnal quietness, and his frantic demands for explanation were at least two decibels lower than usual. Eggart got up wearily to meet him.

"But who done it?" he kept repeating angrily. "They can't get away with it—right under your nose!"

"She did it herself, Cooney."

"You mean she confessed?"

"Not yet—she's too weak to say anything yet. But there's no possible doubt."

"Oh, isn't there! You think they're gonna swallow another suicide? Right on top of Bellane? You think—"

"This is the only suicide."

Something in Eggart's manner checked the other, who looked at his haggard face sharply for a minute and then grumbled, "Well, I want to hear what this is all about. All of it, and right now. I tell you, we got to get organized around here—and fast!" He broke off as a large, stooping figure appeared in the door and fixed his deep eyes, misty as a blind man's, on Eggart. "What's this?"

Eggart stepped forward. "Yes, Mr. Schafft?"

"He says—I think—"

"She's conscious?"

"I don't know—if you'd come ..."

Eggart went past him without a word, and met the doctor in the hall. "Can I see her now?"

"Not just yet, but if you want a statement you might begin to get ready. You understand the nurse and I will have to be present."

"Will she pull through?"

The doctor shrugged and then—an unexpected and somehow disconcerting movement—yawned widely. Eggart's jaw muscles tugged in sympathy, and he clamped his teeth together.

"Sorry. I can't tell you yet. She's lost a lot of blood, and there's the shock factor, hard to calculate. She's pretty old to stand it, but in good physical condition. A lot depends on her—on what help she gives us, you might say."

"If she can speak at all, I've got to see her. Or even if she can understand me."

"You will; I'll do my best for you."

Eggart was left there with Cooney, implacable, at his elbow.

"What were you doing out there in the first place? You didn't say nothing about it to me! You didn't just happen to be there when she picked up a razor!"

"A kitchen knife," Eggart corrected automatically, and there was a sharp sound of breath indrawn behind him. It was the first audible token of his presence that Schafft had given since his loud cry in the cellar, and it seemed to rouse him. He put out his hand and closed it about Eggart's arm, but he said nothing, and after a minute Eggart gently freed himself and returned to Cooney.

"We'd better get Sanders up here, in case we have to move quickly. That's all we need—just Sanders to take down what she says. You and I and the doctor will make plenty of witnesses. And the nurse."

From the discomfited expression on Cooney's face as he turned away, Eggart guessed at hordes of headquarters men inhabiting the waiting room downstairs. But the burly captain was already a little subdued, and he went off down the corridor without reply.

His receding footsteps were crossed with the sound of others, approaching, and presently Bott came in sight, with Edith beside him and Barney a little in the rear. As she caught sight of Schafft, Edith broke away from the others and ran to him.

"Uncle Theo, don't be angry with us for coming—it was horrible just to wait, not to know anything! And I was afraid she—how is she?"

He clung to her but did not answer; it was Bott who stepped up to Eggart and asked, almost humbly, "What is it, Lieutenant? Can't we know anything?"

"Sorry, Bott. We'll all just have to wait." He went beyond him, to the door of the small private room which had been turned over to him, and put one hand on the knob. "You folks can use this room. I'll see that you hear whatever there is to hear."

Barney, white and silent, had remained so nearly outside the room that it took only a step backward, at Eggart's nod, to leave him shut out in the hall with the police officer when the door was closed. Eggart said kindly, "You still in on this, Barney?" and saw him try to speak and fail.

He tried again. "Was it—what I said?"

"Partly, yes. Come on down here, to the end of the hall."

They walked toward the elevator, from which Cooney and another man were getting out.

"You mean it was something about her locking the door, those mornings?"

"She didn't lock it in the morning, Barney. She locked it at night." To Cooney, who was waiting with impatience, he said: "There's a little guy named Bircher waiting down there, too. Maybe somebody ought to keep an eye on him."

"And who's he?"

"Night clerk in the Standish. Sanders, go back down and pass the word on, will you? Don't scare him—just don't let him wander. I don't think he will. The name's Bircher."

"Night clerk at the Standish? You mean he recognized her?"

"No, he didn't. I think he could have, under the proper circumstances, but as it turned out she recognized him first."

"I don't get it. If he doesn't recognize her, what good is he? And what gave you the idea in the first place to—"

"Barney, here," said Eggart. Cooney stared at him as if he had been a new breed of dog. "You remember all that checking we did on Sunday night—trying to trace anybody who'd been out and around in the small hours, and so on? And all the time she was safe inside the hotel, waiting for the morning crowd to cover her, just as the evening crowd had covered her on her way down."

"But you just said the clerk doesn't recognize her— how are you going to prove it? Did somebody else—?"

"The register," said Eggart. "She had to sign the register, to get a room. And it's pretty hard to disguise your handwriting when you've been writing one way for over fifty years. Look, Cooney, let me tell it to you from the beginning, as far as it goes. A few days ago Barney, here, was talking to the Schaffts' maid …"

Under Cooney's apoplectic stare he related the story of the early-morning shopping, the doors locked and unlocked, and Marja and Barney's experiences with them. "At first I thought the peaches were a blind, and that it must be her own absence she wanted to conceal on those particular mornings. But locking the doors only drew attention to her absence, which was otherwise quite usual—*unless it had begun the night before.*"

"How could she stay out all night without any of those people knowing it?"

"She could. She slept downstairs, and the rest of

them upstairs. She was the last to retire, and the first to get up. The only way she could have been missed was if someone had been ill or come to her room in the night. That was the possibility that made her lock her door, and it was ten chances to one that she could unlock it again in the morning with no one the wiser."

"But the house door," said Barney. "Surely she didn't leave that open all night?"

"Why not? From the street it wasn't noticeable until broad daylight, and the neighborhood was a quiet one, as she said herself. What better sign could there be of her having just stepped out that morning, than the house being opened up? I think that was largely for your benefit, Barney, and Marja's."

Cooney was growing impatient.

"All right, so she could have spent the night out. But how do you know she did? Who checked that writing besides you? Why don't the clerk remember her? It was only last night!"

"He does remember her. She was a very respectable old lady, resting between trains, whose luggage was checked at the station. She wore a black coat, hat and gloves, and carried what she needed for the night in a big reticule. That was all there was to her. When she got outside the hotel all she had to do was put the hat and gloves into the reticule, unbutton the coat to show her housedress, and walk into the house looking just as usual, with a bag of peaches bought on the way home."

"And the Clyde?" Barney asked. "Did she stay there too?"

"I haven't checked there yet, but—"

"Then it's time we did," snapped Cooney, and pounced on the unlucky police stenographer who was just getting out of the elevator again. "Sanders, you go on back down and tell Mahaney I want to see him up here."

"You'll need this," Eggart told him, and pulled a twice-folded piece of paper out of his wallet. Cooney unfolded it and gave a smothered yelp.

"Mrs. Mabel Bottman! You mean it's *her?* You mean it's *Bott's* mother in there?"

"No, no—Bott's mother doesn't know anything about this. That's the only writing of Mrs. Schafft's that I had—she gave it to me a few days ago, and it just happened that I kept it. When I got this idea about her staying at the hotel, and thought of checking the register, I remembered her writing this address down for me. All this was after I left you last night. I went right over to the Standish, found out it all checked, and brought the clerk out to the house with me right then. What I hadn't suspected was that the old lady would be so quick. You know how it worked out. I didn't have a chance to call you until we got here."

"And a nice mess you've got for me. The only evidence there is against this Schafft lady is that *you think* her writing matches some writing on the Standish register, and that an old lady stayed there last night. The clerk don't recognize her. She doesn't admit a thing. This locking the door don't mean anything to me yet. Okay; then so far we got two little bits of writing. Is that it?"

"You've got her, with her wrists cut open," said Barney imprudently. Cooney looked at him with stolid dislike.

"You think that's good, do you? You think that's the kind of stuff that gives a police department a good name—hounding an old lady to try and kill herself, after the case is closed? After we've as good as give it out that the fellow who did it is dead? You think if one suicide is good, two must be better?"

"But what if Bellane didn't kill himself?"

Eggart, knowing that at the moment Cooney's main desire was to demonstrate that they were hopelessly situated, made Barney a slight signal to keep quiet. It wasn't necessary; Cooney was through with Barney. He said to Eggart with immense relish,

"I tell you frankly, Eggart, I think you handled this wrong. You jump to conclusions. You ain't satisfied with a case that goes along smooth in one direction—not you. It's got to go in every direction at once, with everybody in town mixed up in it." The elevator brought Sanders up for the third time, with Mahaney just behind him. Cooney ignored them. "I tell you, if this old lady dies without saying what you want her to say, your trouble's just beginning. Her family is going to say she's white as a lamb, and we pushed her till she didn't know what she was doing. And what kind of an answer have we got? A piece of paper, and a hotel clerk that can't say yes or no!"

Eggart said it was a bad lookout, certainly, and that the full responsibility was his; and Cooney was so far appeased as to turn to Mahaney and give him his instructions about checking over the Clyde register for the night of Lenore Bellane's death. After Mahaney left his manner became a little more normal, as if he felt that his own prudence had been established; but it was clear to Barney that he waited with far less patience than Eggart for some word of Mrs. Schafft, and that his expectations of what she might say were no different than his lieutenant's.

"It would be like her to play 'possum," he burst out at one point. "To try and slide out without saying a word! She must know damn' well we can't prove anything without her."

This time Eggart ventured to disagree. "I think we might. Besides, I believe she'll want to speak, if she can. To clear her son of any suspicion of being an accomplice."

"Yeah, there's that. By God, where is he?"

Eggart told him, down the hall in a private room; and Cooney immediately got up to go in search of what small comfort he could find in the son until the mother should be available. Before he got more than a few steps away the figure they had been waiting for came into sight: Mrs. Schafft's doctor, at the other end of the hall. He caught sight of them, and made for them with a rapid, noiseless step. Cooney and Eggart met him halfway. In the hospital hush Barney, who had remained where he was, could plainly hear Cooney's eager: "Now, doctor? You want us now?" And the low reply:

"No, I'm afraid it's no use, officer. I'm sorry. We did what we could, but there was just too much against us."

Eggart said nothing, and Cooney, ramming his hat down over his ears, turned away with a loud groan and said, "I knew it, I knew it!" But this time he was unaware of any audience, and his pessimism was genuine.

Chapter Twenty-one

There was no sleep at the house in Brookline that night. Although it was past midnight when Barney drove them back, although they were all of them stupid with fatigue and shock, Edith was afraid to leave Schafft by himself. Tacitly they remained together, Edith and her silent charge in the living room, and

Bott and Barney, making coffee for them all and drinking their own in silence together, in the kitchen.

The outburst of anger, the immediate defense of his mother's innocence which Cooney had feared, was the least of his worries now if he had known. Schafft's preoccupation was intense and druglike, as if he held tightly to some tenuous line of communication with his dead mother which the others could not share. He sat hunched over on the couch, fists to head, and neither spoke nor moved. Edith was trying to persuade him to lie down, to accept coffee, to speak to her; and the other two thought it best to leave her alone until she either succeeded or acknowledged failure.

Barney, at first impressed by Bott's unusual tact and silence, soon began to be made uneasy by it. He had tried to go upstairs and leave the three of them together, and Bott would not hear of it. He seemed nervous at the idea, and insisted on drawing Barney into the kitchen with him. But once there he fell into unbroken silence; and when their eyes met Bott's slid away at once, with dogged regularity. Barney stood this as long as he could, and then said:

"Do you understand this, Bott? Do you have any idea what we ought to do?"

"I'm an outsider as much as you, feller," Bott replied tersely; and then Barney began to understand. Incredibly, in the midst of all that had happened and that was to come, it was Bott's pride that was suffering. His family, his refined and docile family whose every concern he had known, that he had bound to him by so many ties of obligation and intimacy, had escaped him. As Barney considered, he saw how complete that escape now was.

First there had been Edith, with the suddenly acquired fortune that made her independent of his patronage. That the fortune made, and would have made, almost no difference at all in Edith's attitude to her old friend, Barney sincerely believed; she had been too long used to him; her affection was a habit and a duty. But the difference to Bott was incalculable. He had fully realized his own power, and as fully realized the loss of it. Nothing would convince him that Edith was not lost to him. She was no longer "his." Someone else had outbid him.

But at least he had remained a part of her family, with his old influence over the man who influenced her—Schafft. But now there was no more family. The old lady's amazing defection, whatever had caused it (and Barney saw that, for Bott, this was secondary), split them once and for all into two groups. Their present positions indicated it: Edith and the music teacher alone together, and Bott, with whatever company he could command at the moment, keeping a wary eye on them from a distance. The distance would gradually grow, Barney thought, as Bott's bitterness grew; and Edith would be bewildered for a while, and then would gradually accept what she did not understand....

He was roused from these fancies, which were a half-sleep, by her appearance at the kitchen door. She was pale, but alert; and it seemed to Barney that the change in her had already begun. She was maturing, with decision and responsibility apparent in her already. Just for a second, Barney felt a pang on his own behalf. For a little while he had been her only young friend, the only person her age with entree to her home. Now he was part of something she would only want to forget. But it was too late—and too profitless—to be thinking along those lines. He got up at once.

"What is it, Edith?"

"Oh, Barney, I think we'd better get him upstairs to bed. I can stay with him there, and he must rest...."

They went into the living room together, followed after a moment by Bott, treasuring his first slight. She had forgotten to speak to him at all.

Barney said, "Rest wouldn't hurt you, either. Let me sit up with him for a while."

Unexpectedly, Schafft spoke for himself. "Edith, don't leave me. Don't leave me."

"I won't, dearest. Not ever. Can you stand up if we help you?"

"Just come with me. I'm all right."

But he let Barney draw one arm over his shoulder, and Edith took the other. He was weaker than he thought, or would own, and the way upstairs was long. Halfway up Bott offered to relieve Edith, but she said "Oh, no, Bott—let me!" and he nodded, with a tight smile, and stepped back.

Schafft was stretched out on his own wide bed, and Barney made Edith lie down there too. Schafft, with Edith's hand in his, turned his head away at once and appeared to lose consciousness of them both, and of Bott in the doorway. Barney waited a minute beside the bed, with Edith's wide eyes turned up to him.

"Go to bed, Barney," she whispered. "You're tired, too."

"I'll leave my door open, and this one. If you call me I'll hear you."

"All right. Thank you, Barney."

At the door Bott gave him a long look before turning away to cross the hall and shut himself in his own room. "You, too," the look said. "You're something else between us, I see." He did not answer Barney's good night. But Barney had walked too long on the precarious footing of Bott's goodwill to be depressed at losing it now. If he fires me, he fires me, he thought, and stopped at his own door to fasten it wide open.

He undressed in the dark, with a little awkward groping, and at one point put his hand into something distinctly unpleasant. With a stifled exclamation he switched the smallest light on and held up his fingers; they were coated with a pale yellow substance that left him appalled until it occurred to him to sniff at it. Then remembrance was sudden and complete. The pudding. The peace offering, brought him only a few hours ago by the woman who was now dead. He went in the bathroom and washed, feeling more shaken than he had since their return to the house.

The neglected dish somehow brought everything into perspective which had been blurred by shock and many small events. He realized how few hours had gone by since Mrs. Schafft had come to his room, and that she would certainly never come again. Whatever urgency had moved her then, she had left it behind her now.

He came back into his room, wakeful, lit a cigarette, and moved about in restless silence. The visit had begun to oppress him. She must have been more desperate than he had known, to be driven into such a useless and trivial errand. And then to come downstairs and find Eggart there, with the Standish night clerk ...

But was her interest in him trivial, after all? She had not known at that time that Eggart's suspicions were in any way centered on her, or that any proof against her could be produced. As far as she knew, the only people who doubted her at all were Marja, and through Marja, himself. The maid had been silenced by removing her to a place where her vague opinions could do no harm, but if Barney were to become a kind of "carrier" for those opinions—were to hear and believe them?

From her point of view, Barney could see that he might have been, perhaps, a very real concern to the old lady. The trouble was that even with all his former wondering, there had been lacking that ingredient of real belief in a real guilt which would have made him take her as seriously as he should have. She was not, as she had seemed, a fretful old lady who pried without reason and distributed pudding to excuse herself. She was a woman of extraordinary resolve and daring, who did what she had to however she could.

He told himself this, seeing from what had happened that it must be true; and yet, that real belief was still absent. She still occupied his mind as old Mrs. Schafft, who made pudding. The dish sat beside him, more real than any rumor of guilt. He picked it up, stuck an experimental finger in it, and put the finger in his mouth. The next minute, with ludicrous care, he took it out again, with its coating as nearly undisturbed as possible. A light sweat broke out on his forehead, and he got up immediately and went into the bathroom to wash his finger clean again—and to rinse out his mouth.

When he came back, his whole conception of Mrs. Schafft had altered to fit reason instead of memory. He had tasted nothing, felt nothing; the change was purely a product of his mind, and an atavistic physical alertness.

She had not given him the pudding until *after* their talk; until he had completely failed to satisfy her. He picked the dish up and carried it over under the light. The yellow surface, except where he had broken it, had congealed to smoothness; it seemed to him that there were white particles, too tiny for beaten egg, distributed over it. And through it. What?

There was one sure way to find out. Eggart, even in the midst of his own trouble—perhaps because of it—would certainly arrange for an analysis. If what Barney half suspected were true, Mrs. Schafft would not have died with such discretion after all. There would be one certain witness left to testify against her.

While he stood there a faint sound reached him from the next room. He thought it was his name, said very low in Edith's voice; but when he went to stand in the doorway and whisper, "What? Did you call me?" there was no reply.

He waited a little longer, and then returned to stand in his own doorway in the same attitude of indecision. Then, moving very silently and quickly, he took up the little dish again and carried it into the bathroom, where he washed its contents away with hot water, and then polished the dish itself until it shone.

Chapter Twenty-two

What Eggart went through in the next twenty-odd hours, between Cooney and his own conscience, was not known to anyone but himself. He did his best to fill in the story which death had left so blank. The modest, train-traveling old lady's presence in both the Clyde and the Standish was definitely established, for the nights on which Lenore Bellane and her brother-in-law had died. Her photograph, retouched to include the black hat found in her reticule, was tentatively identified at both hotels; the handwriting experts were given every scrap of her writing that could be collected to compare with the two hotel signatures.

It was a far from hopeless case, judged on its merits alone; but the trouble was that the Bellane case had not so far been conducted according to evidence but on a kind of newspaper-release sensationalism which now found itself confused and suspicious since the apparent non sequitur of a second suicide.

On the late afternoon of the following day Eggart, looking in at his office briefly, found Mahaney and an elderly man in excited conference in the outer office. The conference had clearly just begun; Mahaney was not sure of the man's name, nor he of Mahaney's authority; but they had managed to infect each other with some excitement that made them both incoherent.

"Jeez, I was praying you'd show up!" Mahaney exclaimed as Eggart walked in the door. "Look, this guy—this is the undertaker, see? The old lady's undertaker! He's got her clothes, see, and—"

"My name is Thorpe," the other interrupted. "James T. Thorpe. This is my card. I should like to be taken to whoever is in charge of the Schafft case. I can produce credentials—"

"That isn't necessary, Mr. Thorpe. Will you come in my office? I'm Lieutenant Eggart, and this is Sergeant Mahaney. What can we do for you?"

"I think, Lieutenant," said Mr. Thorpe, bursting his dam, "that I am going to be able to do something for *you*. I hope so. You understand that I have not read the entire document—I did not feel that I was entitled to. But—"

"What document is this, Mr. Thorpe?"

For answer, the undertaker slowly uncovered and handed to Eggart a small, folded tobacco pouch of oiled silk. "Found," he said impressively, "pinned to her corset-cover. With two pins."

Eggart took one glance at the dimly discernible lines of writing, visible through the silk, and felt the blood leave his head. He couldn't help it. It meant too much—there was no use pretending that it didn't. Carefully he lifted the flap, drew out the folded sheets of paper inside, and read the first paragraph. Then he lowered the hand that held the papers, feeling it tremble slightly, and said:

"You're right, Mr. Thorpe. This is a most important find, and we can't be grateful enough to you for bringing it directly here. I suppose you *have* brought it here first?"

"Certainly, sir. I and one assistant are the only two people who know of its existence, and I think you will find that we have been as quick and quiet about getting it to you as—"

"I know you have. Our sincere thanks to you for doing your duty in a splendid manner. I know the Commissioner will want to write to you about it. And right now, of course, you'll want a receipt...."

Hardly knowing what he said or did, Eggart wrote the receipt, repeated every complimentary expression of thanks he could think of, and gradually made it clear to Mr. Thorpe that he was *not* expected to stay for the reading. The undertaker finally went away in a mixture of disappointment and excited virtue, and Mahaney locked the door behind him instantly. He came up to Eggart's desk voluble with triumph, and found the lieutenant already oblivious of him. He was reading silently, intensely, as if his life depended on it. In a manner of speaking, it almost did.

Mahaney, who was fond of his superior in moments of agreement, sat down in indulgent silence and waited for the top sheet to fall to his hand. It was a long time in coming, but he decided, after two lines, it had been worth waiting for. It began without salutation or date:

"If this is read by my son or any member of my family or their agents, I ask them to destroy it unread. If it has come to the hands of the persons for whom it is meant, the information desired begins on the following page."

As a matter of fact, it began on the back of that one, as Mahaney discovered by turning it over. Again the beginning was abrupt.

"I am the sole person responsible for the death of Lenore Bellane Schafft, the wife of my son, and the sole person who has any private knowledge of her death. No one but myself knows anything of what I have done, or has given me any assistance in doing it. As proof that what I say is true, I shall give an account of all my actions and keep it on my person where it must be found if I should meet with an accident.

"This woman, on Sunday, the 16th of August, at about 5:30 in the afternoon, came to me in the kitchen of my home and told me in confidence that she had just asked my son to give her a divorce, and that he had refused. She wanted my help in persuading him to change his mind. I told her I would not give it. She then told me that while she was fond of my son (this was not true) and did not wish to harm him (she had harmed him in every possible way for eleven years), there were circumstances making a divorce very necessary. She said she knew that I was a calm and reasonable woman, and that my son listened to my advice; and then told me of a private circumstance which I shall not write here, to convince me of the justice of her request.

"I knew Lenore too well to believe all that she chose to say was true, without proof; but the possibility that she might be speaking the truth now disturbed me very greatly. I was inclined for reasons which I will not go into to believe that she was in earnest, and that my son now had, unknown to himself, a wealthy and determined enemy who would not only bring disgrace and public shame upon him but would deprive him of the little joy he had left in life since his marriage. I said nothing of this to Lenore, but only told her I could not answer her at such short notice, and would need further time and explanation first. Since it was not possible for us to have a long private talk in my home without the others being aware of it, which Lenore wished no more than I, she asked me if I would be willing to come to her hotel room the following day. I said I would, and she gave me the number of her room and appointed a time. Shortly after this she left our house.

"I had no intention, from the first, of pleading or attempting to change her mind. Given Lenore's character, and if what she had told me were true, I knew it would be useless. I knew I must find another way to change her plans. By nine that night I had come to the decision that only her death would answer the purpose.

"I had then, and have now, no feeling that her life was necessary to anyone, or her death any loss to the world. The only thing that troubled me was that I did not know how to kill her. I am a strong woman, but she was far younger than I, and I did not wish for any struggle or outcry that would involve me, and hence my son, in public trouble. I knew that she had been in the habit of taking a sleeping medicine containing veronal while she lived in our home, and that this was a longstanding habit. It occurred to me that if I could be with her during the night, while she was under its influence, I would have less difficulty with her.

If I could manage to see that she had an unusually strong dose, the problem might even solve itself, and her death would appear a suicide. I decided to try that night.

"As soon as my household had gone to bed I put on my coat and hat, locked the doors to my bedroom, and left the house, leaving the front door open for a reason which I shall presently explain. I went downtown by trolley, arriving at the Clyde shortly after eleven, and went directly to the desk where I engaged a room for the night in a name that is not my own. I went up to this room and remained there only a few moments; then I took the stairway down to Lenore's floor, which was below mine, and knocked on her door.

"She was up, as I had expected, and was even then writing a letter to my son. I told her that I would not have been able to come the next day and thought it better to come that night, and she seemed perfectly satisfied. She seemed pleased to see me, as she said she was nervous and impatient about the delay. She at once entered into a long explanation of her personal history, and showed me an early letter from the person with whom she was in league against my son. I listened to her for over an hour, without betraying my own feelings at her behavior, and finally told her that I would talk to my son and get in touch with her. I advised her to go to bed and put the affair out of her mind. She said she was too upset to sleep, from so much crying (she had been crying as she talked), and I asked her if she had nothing to take. It was perfectly easy. I put her to bed, and at her direction found her sleeping powders in the bathroom. She instructed me to use one, and I used three. I was afraid that any more would have too strong a taste. She drank the medicine and lay down. I promised to sit with her until she should sleep, and she seemed grateful.

"I did sit beside her until the powders took effect, which was not long, and then continued to wait until they should take further effect. By 12:30 I was convinced that the dose had been too small. I did not know what to do. By now I had determined that her death must appear to be suicide, but I could think of no other means to use. I went into the bathroom and drew a tub of water, intending to carry her to it; but while she did not recover consciousness when I tried to lift her, I was not strong enough.

"The implement which I finally used was her own, and I found it in her traveling bag. I removed my outer clothing to use it, and also protected my hands and arms with the sheet. When I left the room she was still alive, but I was convinced that she would not be so by an hour from that time.

"I went upstairs to my own room, once more removed my outer clothing, and ascertained that the few stains on my other garments could be easily removed. I removed them. I had previously rinsed out Lenore's glass, mixed a new and smaller dose of bromide, and poured most of it down the sink, putting the glass back at her side. I had also taken away with me the letter I had seen, but had left the one to my son, since it seemed appropriate, and was not addressed to him by name. During my entire visit to her room I had worn my black cotton gloves, to avoid leaving the personal traces which everyone now knows of, and the gloves were in very poor condition and stained. I shredded them as well as I could and disposed of them in my room. The number of this room was 943, and I was registered under the name of Mrs. Harriet Stanley.

"At six-thirty I was called by the desk, in order to

catch a train as they believed, and I then left the hotel. I took the trolley to the market near my home, purchased three pounds of peaches, and walked to my house. It was then, as I had planned, a little after 7:30.

My maid would be in the kitchen; the open front door would tell her that I had gone to market, so that she would not be surprised at my appearance. I had put my hat in my reticule, as I was not accustomed to wear it in the neighborhood. The rest of my household does not rise until eight.

"I entered the open front door, went to my room by way of the music parlor, and unlocked the door. In my room I removed my coat and unmade my bed. I then unlocked the other door of my room from the inside, and came out into the dining room. My maid unfortunately happened to be in that room at the time I did so, but as she is not accustomed to question my actions or to think much on any subject, I was not much concerned.

"This is the entire story. It will be apparent that I neither had nor needed any help in what I have done, nor have I any regret."

On the same page, but with some difference in the quality of ink and writing that indicated a break in time, a new paragraph began:

"It is necessary for me to reopen this packet, and to add that the death of Francis Bellane is also my sole responsibility, although not entirely my doing. His own fear of me is greatly to blame. I had no thought of harm to him when he came to my house, since I believed that without Lenore's help, his evil plans against my son could come to nothing. His own actions convinced me that this was not true; he was wary of us all—of me particularly, I believe—and yet his persist-

ence in appearing in our home, his carelessness of
what we would make of his behavior there, convinced
me that he had some secret weapon against us. I
learned after Lenore's death that he had been in
Boston, in the hotel itself, not many hours before my
visit; I understood that there was some doubt of his
having returned to New York that evening. Whether
or not he had, I had no assurance that Lenore had not
told him of seeking my help—perhaps even of my
promised visit to her room. It was necessary for me to
talk with him alone.

"The procedure I had followed with Lenore was the
only convenient one for me to use in leaving my house
without my family's knowledge. I knew his hotel, and
engaged a room there, also, for the simple reason that
I did not wish to return to my own home at the late
hour that would be necessary, since I could not start
downtown until nearly eleven. Merely as a precaution
I used an entirely different name, that of Mrs. Louise
Brown, and I occupied Room 312. I had no intention
of violence when I came to his room, nor had I any
weapon. I think this will answer for the innocence of
my intentions, since he was far larger and stronger
appearing than I.

"I used as my excuse a private desire to talk with
him about his reasons for remaining in Boston, and
his future plans as they affected our family. I have
never had any difficulty in gaining a certain amount
of trust and confidence from any person to whom I
particularly apply, and Mr. Bellane's clear distrust
and nervousness made me sure that Lenore had told
him something to make him suspicious. He was not
willing to receive me; he would neither sit down nor
close his door, and when I closed it myself he went to
the far end of the room from my chair and seated

himself on the window sill. I presently observed that the window was wide open behind him, and I was aware that it gave on a paved courtyard.

"In order to engage his attention I made it clear that I knew of all his private affairs and I further told him several family matters (some of them not true) which I thought would astonish him. His interest having for the moment made him forget his distrust, I was able to walk up to him and say that finally, I was forced to trust him with a piece of knowledge that no one else shared, and would ask for his promise of secrecy. At this point I allowed my gloves to drop, stooped for them at once, and grasping both his feet raised them as high as I could and pushed. He attempted to catch at the window frame, but was unsuccessful.

"I immediately returned to Room 312, from the windows of which I could well see the courtyard, and spent the night there. In the morning I returned to my home, where I learned that the fall had not been immediately fatal. What this will mean to me, I do not yet know. However, for my son's sake, this document must continue in existence until it is no longer necessary."

Eggart had finished his reading some time before Mahaney, but there was no sign of impatience from his side of the desk. He sat with his forehead braced on his hand, and stared down thoughtfully at his blotter. It was Mahaney, finally, who broke the silence, as he put back the final sheet.

"What the newspapers wouldn't give for this!" he exclaimed. "Some old lady! Talk about Dracula!"

"Let's not," said Eggart. "We'll save Dracula for a quieter day." He smiled with an effort, and got up. "Right now we'd better get hold of Cooney, and start this on its way around."

Mahaney rose with alacrity. "And boy, will it leave smoke in its trail! I guess we were plenty right this time, hey, Lieutenant?"

"In a way."

Even then, doubt could still seize on Mahaney when he looked at Eggart's face.

"It's what you wanted, ain't it?"

Eggart gathered the sheets carefully together, and walked over to unlock his door.

"As long as I'm a policeman, it sure is," he said. "Come on, Mahaney."

THE END

E. P. Fenwick was born Elizabeth Jane Phillips on April 5, 1916 in St. Louis, Missouri. After high school, she wrote poetry and an unpublished first

novel which she destroyed when it was rejected by a publisher. She then enrolled in secretarial courses and became a French translator for two years. She adopted the pseudonym E. P. Fenwick in the early 1940s and resumed writing, publishing three detective

mysteries with Farrar, Rinehart. After turning to mainstream writing for ten years as Elizabeth Fenwick, she returned to writing crime fiction with the suspense novel *Poor Harriet*. Fenwick married noted harpsichord maker, David Jacques Way, in 1950, and continued to publish more suspense novels until 1973. She died from Alzheimer's Disease on November 20, 1996.

BLACK GAT BOOKS

Black Gat Books is an exciting line of mass market paperbacks introduced in 2015 by Stark House Press. New titles appear every two months, featuring the best in crime fiction reprints. Each book is sized to 4.25" x 7", just like they used to be. Collect them all! $9.99 each.

1 Haven for the Damned
by Harry Whittington
978-1-933586-75-5

2 Eddie's World
by Charlie Stella
978-1-933586-76-2

3 Stranger at Home
by Leigh Brackett
writing as George Sanders
978-1-933586-78-6

4 The Persian Cat
by John Flagg
978-1933586-90-8

5 Only the Wicked
by Gary Phillips
978-1-933586-93-9

6 Felony Tank
by Malcolm Braly
978-1-933586-91-5

7 The Girl on the Bestseller List
by Vin Packer
978-1-933586-98-4

8 She Got What She Wanted by Orrie Hitt
978-1-944520-04-5

9 The Woman on the Roof
by Helen Nielsen
978-1-944520-13-7

10 Angel's Flight
by Lou Cameron
978-1-944520-18-2

11 The Affair of Lady Westcott's Lost Ruby / The Case of the Unseen Assassin by Gary Lovisi
978-1-944520-22-9

Stark House Press

1315 H Street, Eureka, CA 95501 707-498-3135
griffinskye3@sbcglobal.net www.starkhousepress.com

Available from your local bookstore or direct from the publisher.

Malice Domestic

Classic Women's Suspense from the 1940s & 50s

Elisabeth Sanxay Holding
Widow's Mite / Who's Afraid
978-1-944520-34-2 $19.95
Two suspense classics from the
author of *The Blank Wall*.
"The author has succeeded
admirably in depicting the mounting
horror and suspense." —*NY Times*.
Introduction by Gregory Shepard.

Jean Potts
Go, Lovely Rose / The Evil Wish
978-1-944520-65-6 $19.95
A 1954 Edgar Award winner and a
1963 Edgar runner-up paired
together for the first time.
"If Hitchcock had written a novel, it
would have been similar to *The Evil
Wish*...two masterpieces."
—Don Crinklaw, *Booklist*. New
introduction by J. F. Norris.

Helen Nielsen
Borrow the Night / The Fifth Caller
978-1-944520-72-4 $19.95
Two vintage Southern California
mysteries from the author of *The
Woman on the Roof*.
"A skillfully devised and movingly
presented drama of sin, retribution,
and supreme sacrifice."
—*Chicago Tribune*. New introduction
by Nicholas Litchfield.

Bernice Carey
The Man Who Got Away With It /
The Three Widows
978-1-944520-80-9 $19.95
"Carey... was an adept plotter but
was more interested in
characterization and social
comment...very much a forerunner of
modern *literary* crime fiction."
— Xavier Lechard, *At the Villa Rose*.
"A powerful psychological drama
written with great literary flair."
—Nicholas Litchfield. New
introduction by Curtis Evans.

Dolores Hitchens
Stairway to an Empty Room / Terror
Lurks in Darkness
978-1-944520-79-3 $19.95
Two terrific crime novels from the
author of *Sleep With Strangers*.
"High-grade suspense."
—*San Francisco Chronicle*.
"Expertly tautened action and
style."—*Saturday Review*. New
introduction by Nicholas Litchfield.

Coming Soon: Home is the
Prisoner/The Little Lie—*Jean Potts*
Footsteps in the Dark/Beat Back the
Tide—*Dolores Hitchens*
The Body on the Sidewalk/The
Reluctant Murderer—*Bernice Carey*

Stark House Press

1315 H Street, Eureka, CA 95501 707-498-3135
griffinskye3@sbcglobal.net www.starkhousepress.com

Available in trade paperback from the publisher, Ingram or Baker & Taylor Books.

Made in the USA
Columbia, SC
22 October 2020